G000271085

Sara Sheeran was born in London, England but has lived in Ireland for the past twenty-seven years. She is a qualified Early Years Professional. Sara is married with three children.

For my family. Thank you for your love and support.

Sara Sheeran

THE SUM OF ALL PARTS

AUSTIN MACAULEY PUBLISHERS™

LONDON • CAMBRIDGE • NEW YORK • SHARJAH

Copyright © Sara Sheeran 2023

The right of Sara Sheeran to be identified as author of this work has been asserted by the author in accordance with sections 77 and 78 of the Copyright, Designs and Patents Act 1988.

All rights reserved. No part of this publication may be reproduced, stored in a retrieval system, or transmitted in any form or by any means, electronic, mechanical, photocopying, recording, or otherwise, without the prior permission of the publishers.

Any person who commits any unauthorised act in relation to this publication may be liable to criminal prosecution and civil claims for damages.

This is a work of fiction. Names, characters, businesses, places, events, locales, and incidents are either the products of the author's imagination or used in a fictitious manner. Any resemblance to actual persons, living or dead, or actual events is purely coincidental.

A CIP catalogue record for this title is available from the British Library.

ISBN 9781398485150 (Paperback)
ISBN 9781398485167 (ePub e-book)

www.austinmacauley.com

First Published 2023
Austin Macauley Publishers Ltd®
1 Canada Square
Canary Wharf
London
E14 5AA

Table of Contents

It has been said: the whole is greater than the sum of its parts.
It is more correct to say that the whole is other than the sum of
its parts, because summing up is a meaningless procedure,
whereas the whole-part relationship is meaningful.

Kurt Koffka

Our life is what our thoughts make it.

Marcus Aurelius

I
The End of the Beginning

Thoughts

I am lost. I am weary. There is only birth and death, and in between—what is there? Only love and pain and regret.

I want to go back, right back to the beginning, and start afresh. But I can't of course. None of us can. I examine and analyse my every thought and my every decision, and I relive my past. I focus on the minutiae, on every detail and every aspect of my existence. I rebuild my childhood home over and over again in my mind so as never to forget.

I retrace my steps. I remember the sounds and the smells and the sights: the feel of the smooth wooden banister under the palm of my hand and the creak of the third step on the stair; the musical "chink" of that one paving stone on the garden path that always alerted us to visitors; the musty smell of wood and damp in my father's shed; the way my mother would always hold my hand as we walked and gently stroke it to soothe away my worries.

My childhood. My childhood home. Gone now. No doubt it has changed beyond recognition. The beautiful garden razed, the garden where I spent so many happy hours playing amongst the flowers—the hollyhock and phlox whose blossoms I would use as hats for my dolls, the blues and pinks of the tiny forget-me-nots, the secluded bower where I would sit in sweet reverie. It is all gone.

I am officially homeless now. I simply exist in this house; I do not live. It is not a home, not truly.

My childhood. My youth. My land of lost content. A place to which I can never return. But in my thoughts, I find that, yes, I can. There, in the safety and sanctuary of my mind, I relive every past moment, I explore my father's garden, I visit every room of my childhood, and I search every corner.

I don't want to forget.

The Wife

She lay on the bed staring blankly up at the ceiling, tracing the cracks and the cobwebs in the dim glow of the streetlamp that had found its way in through the crack in the curtains. Yet another night of broken sleep. She loved him, didn't

13

she? And yet it was only at night, when they made love, that she felt any real connection to him. Then he was her one true love in all his glory. At all other times, he was just there. But even that connection seemed to be diminishing. Lovemaking was fewer and farther between, and excuses were made—too tired, a headache, too hot, too cold. The usual litany. Instead, intimacy and passion were being steadily replaced with perfunctory kisses on the cheek and murmured goodnights.

It was just the two of them again now. Their daughter was all grown up and had embarked on her own adventures, her first foray into adult life. They had always said that this would be "their time", that they would make the most of the solitude and recapture their lost youth and rekindle their romance. They would finally get that honeymoon. It was meant to be a new chapter in their lives, but instead, it felt like the book was ending and she felt overwhelmingly lost and alone.

The lines of communication were most definitely down. He had begun to find solace in a pint glass and said that he didn't want to talk about it. And she was far from perfect. She had never been able to express her feelings, preferring to bottle them up inside, letting them slowly burn and corrode her until she had no feelings left at all. Perhaps if he knew how she felt—how lonely, how unloved, how unfulfilled—then something could be done. But whenever the opportunity arose to discuss their marriage, she always kept quiet. Why rock the boat when they were already in stormy waters? She wanted to ask if he had found someone else, but something always stopped her and held her back. What if he said yes? Is that what she wanted, an easy way out, herself blameless and guilt-free? But what would happen to her in that scenario? Despite everything she did not want to be alone. He had always been there, he was her entire life, and yet now separation seemed likely, and divorce had even been mentioned. The spectre of divorce now loomed constantly in the shadows filling her with dread and anxiety. She felt so confused and hopeless, but if she were completely honest there was also the tiniest amount of hope, of release, of freedom, and that also scared and exhilarated her. Yet despite everything, she could not bear the thought of life without him.

But she already was without him. It was two in the morning and still no sign of him coming home. She slipped out of bed and into her dressing gown, secreting her mobile phone in its pocket, and padded down the stairs.

The Woman

I just saw your lovely face.
You're sweet. I knew there was a reason I liked you.
Can you get away?
No.
Story of your life. Left locked in the tower. You need a Prince Charming.
Where would I find one of those?
I'm in the pub. A bit wasted though.
No thanks. I prefer my men sober and healthy.

Thoughts

They say that everyone has a book inside them. But unfortunately, not everyone is a writer. I live through books. It is how I learn, how I travel, how I console myself. In fact, it would be fair to say that my best friends tend to be of the paperback variety—hardback if I can afford it. A type of literary prostitution.

I am perceived as odd, I know this, and I don't particularly mind. Not anymore. Weird is good. No not weird, I am unique: a limited edition.

I have intense mood swings. One minute I am euphoric and the next I am in tears. And I am quiet to the point of sullenness. I am withdrawn. Look up the word "introvert" in the dictionary and you will find my name next to it.

But remember, it is the quiet ones that you have to watch.

The Girl

3 July

Dear Diary,
He asked me out at last! He is so adorable! We went to the cinema, we held hands and he asked if he could kiss me! I've never kissed anyone before. Of course, I messed it up. I was so embarrassed.
Anyway, it's getting late, and I am in desperate need of my beauty sleep.

X

10 July

Dear Diary,

All I do is think about him and how gorgeous he is. That smile…but I saw him in town today with another girl. They were kissing. I feel angry, hurt and stupid. I don't normally trust people, but I chose to trust him. I honestly thought he cared about me. He asked me out so why was he with her? I should have known better than to think—to believe—that he would want to be with me. I obviously have a lot of growing up to do. I am so naïve.

X

11 July

Dear Diary,

Maybe it wasn't him yesterday? Maybe there's an innocent explanation? I should confront him, but I don't want to make an even bigger fool of myself by letting him know how much I like him and how gullible I have been in believing that he felt the same way.

No doubt when I look back on this, I'll be embarrassed, and the importance of the situation will have been lost. But at the moment it matters, and I could really do with some advice. I wish that there was someone that I could talk to.

I really like him, and he told me that he feels the same way. I honestly thought that we would end up with a good relationship—I wasn't kidding myself that it would be permanent, but I did think that it would last longer than a week. I don't know what to do. I suppose I should get some sleep, but I don't think that I could—my mind is working overtime.

I probably was asking for it. I probably did something wrong. Maybe it was that kiss. I half expected something like this would happen. I mean, why would someone as gorgeous as him want someone like me? It's better that it happened now before I got too emotionally attached.

The thing is he seemed such a nice and caring person. He made me feel that I mattered to him. Maybe I'm too innocent and too much of a romantic. If he did have genuine feelings for me, he wouldn't have kissed someone else.

I can't get him out of my head though. I don't want to lose him.

X

13 July

Dear Diary,

It can't have been him that I saw. I've been thinking about it, and it just can't have been. I was quite far away, and they say everyone has a doppelganger, don't they? That would explain things.

Anyhow, it's not as if we're in a serious relationship. I really like him, but he is my first boyfriend—I'm new to all this. And we're not exactly suited. Still, I'm happy with what we've got—which isn't a lot admittedly—stilted, embarrassed conversations; meaningful stares; clumsy kisses!

X

16 July

Dear Diary,

I really do need to talk to him. I agreed to go out with him not just because I'm physically attracted to him but because I want to know him as a person too. If he just wants the physical side, then there's really no point. I don't think that I'm ready for sex. And besides, sex should be with your life partner, shouldn't it?

I saw him this morning and basically, we couldn't keep our hands off each other. Okay, so I wasn't exactly discouraging him...I think a serious talk would be a good idea.

I could see him tomorrow after school, but I think a little breathing space might be needed.

X

20 July

Dear Diary,

We have had a slight disagreement.

Things started to get out of control if you know what I mean—touching and hands where they shouldn't be. I was honest with him and said that I didn't really want to as it made me feel cheap and as if I was being used...

He was angry—offended.

I told him about my paranoia and my inability to trust. He told me that he really likes me and that he wants to take care of me. So, I think the situation is sorted out. He said that he was glad that I had been honest and that he didn't want to lose me over this. I said that there was no danger of that.

X

2 August

Dear Diary,

Life is pretty horrendous at the minute, basically because I don't know what to do with it. I find myself getting really down one minute and almost over excited the next. I can't concentrate and I feel scared. The only time that I feel truly secure and happy is when I'm with him.

We had a lovely time together today, although I suppose initially it wasn't so great because I said I didn't want to go to the pub tonight, so he decided that I was ashamed to be seen with him. We managed to sort things out though, and he even gave me a set of keys to his place! We spent the evening together, watching TV, chatting, and kissing. He said that he likes me "more than a lot"! I think that he was trying to say that he loves me! Part of me is glad that he didn't say it, and part of me is sad. If he had said that he loves me, I would have either not believed him and so hurt him or believed him and I would end up hurt. Worse still, if he had said that he loves me, I might have said that I loved him too. And I only think that I love him. I don't know for sure. I mean how do you know something like that? What is love really anyway? All I do know is that I can't stop thinking about him; I'm insanely jealous and paranoid for no good reason; and when I am with him, I just want him to hold me and to look after me. I feel so close to him—connected. I don't know what I'd do without him.

X

10 August

Dear Diary,

We had an argument today. He came over and we were kissing, and things got a little heated…which was fine…at first. But then it felt wrong—not him, me. So I put a stop to things. It's hard to explain how I felt, but I was scared and felt

ashamed and dirty even though I wanted to…I tried to explain this to him, but it came out all wrong. He said I obviously didn't care about him. He refused to talk to me, to look at me or touch me.

I don't know what to do.

X

12 August

Dear Diary

I saw him yesterday. He wouldn't speak to me at first, apparently he thought that I was going to dump him. He said that he thought that it didn't look as if we were going to last long together. It worried me when he said that and made me panic. I told him that seeing as he was so determined that we wouldn't last, then we probably wouldn't…

Things did improve though and the rest of the afternoon was great. Although in retrospect him undoing my shirt was a little worrying. But then it really is no different to when he puts his hands inside my top. Maybe I should be worrying about that too?

What I would really like to be able to do is to show off my gorgeous man. To show everyone that I am not a stuck-up nerd and boring and quiet. To show that someone thinks I am special. Silly I know.

I am definitely too attached to him. Obsessed. I just hope I don't lose him yet. I know I will eventually, but I need him now.

X

19 August

Dear Diary,

Yesterday was a day of mega embarrassment. I was at his place, and everything was fine—we were chatting, we kissed and cuddled—but things got well and truly out of hand. It was both our faults. I should have told him to stop but I didn't. I guess I didn't want to.

Anyway, I ended up telling him to stop only when we were both half-naked. I have never felt so stupid and so much of a slut in my entire life. I guess I

shouldn't feel this way as I wouldn't have let him get so far if I didn't really care about him, love him maybe…

And it's not as if I wasn't enjoying myself. But it gets to a certain point and I get incredibly nervous. Scared. I feel dirty. It all feels wrong. He was sweet about the whole thing. I said I was sorry, and he said that I needn't apologise. He said that he felt stupid, and he wanted to know how I really felt about him. And this is where I got myself into another embarrassing situation: I told him that I loved him.

I was so scared that he would laugh at me, but he said that he felt the same way. Then he asked me if I'd ever go all the way with him, and I said that I didn't know—possibly. He said he wanted a "yes" or a "no". So I said yes, even though I'm scared.

X

24 August

Dear Diary,

I don't know quite how to put this. I don't have it sorted in my mind yet. I'm a little confused.

Yesterday afternoon, I went to see him and things—well, we got carried away. Again. I actually went over hoping to sleep with him. A combination of curiosity and lust. But I didn't quite carry it through. It was all a bit of a shambles. We were both fully undressed. The whole situation seemed so silly, so ungainly. Plus, I was petrified. I didn't want that thing inside me. So I asked him to stop.

He was very good about it, but it was so awkward. I felt so embarrassed. When he asked why I had told him to stop, I didn't explain—I couldn't. He got a bit pissed off then.

He says that he still cares about me, but we have to talk. So this afternoon that's what we're going to do. Talk. It should be interesting. I do really care about him, I'm just so confused.

X

25 August

Dear Diary,

We didn't exactly talk yesterday but I did tell him that I stopped because I was scared and nervous and not because I didn't like him.

He told me that I was lovely and that he'd like us to be locked up together forever!

We had a beautiful afternoon together, snuggled up, my head on his chest listening to his heartbeat.

X

31 August

Dear Diary,

He's given me the opportunity of seeing him all day, every day! He's asked me to move in with him!

I told him that I wasn't ready for that, that I'm too young. It's a huge step. I was tempted, but maybe I'm too old-fashioned and too romantic—I would have preferred a proposal first. I didn't tell him that obviously!

Of course, when I said no, he got defensive and sulky. He said that we were too opposite and that we were drifting apart. He also said that he thinks he's not good enough for me and that he won't be able to give me everything that I want.

I don't want anything! What do I care so long as I have him?

X

2 September

Dear Diary,

Last night I lost my virginity.

We went out for a few drinks and then went back to his place. He asked me to sleep with him. I said no because neither of us were sober. When I said "no", he said that he loved me, but I obviously didn't love him. He was horrible. The things he said to me, I can't even bear to write it all down. But then he started crying. What can I say? I'm a sucker for tears.

It was so clumsy and awkward. No connection, no feeling other than pain and shame. He guided me through the whole thing like it was a bizarre biology practical—"that's it, hold it like that and now move your hand up and down, that's it, good girl". He said I had to move my body more.

It was so humiliating.

He said that I have a great body and that I'm all that he ever wanted. But I have never experienced so much pain. I didn't enjoy it at all.

He now thinks that he can't satisfy me and that there's no point in us staying together. But he says he loves me. He says he loves me and I'm all that he has.

He says that he never meant to hurt me. I knew we should have waited. If we had waited, it would have meant something. As it is, it meant nothing. I can't help but worry that last night signifies the beginning of the end.

X

II
Remember When

The Girl

13 September

Dear Diary,

He's moving away. He has a new job. It's so far away. I told him that I didn't want him to go, that I didn't want to lose him, and he said that I'd get over him. What the fuck does he know?

He kissed me then and I just started crying. He held me. He was so tender, so gentle. He said if he had realised how much I felt for him he would never have considered accepting the new job. I told him I love him—and I do—and he said he loves me too. I believe him.

He is so beautiful. I wish I were with him now.

X

17 September

Dear Diary,

I went to see him yesterday. I had a great time and I felt really close to him—he told me all about his childhood, his family, and the things he used to get up to. I stayed over and we had sex. And this is when the problems seemed to start again. I wasn't really into it; I didn't want to. I didn't really enjoy it. So he got all grouchy. He said that we should break up even though he says that he loves me more than anyone or anything. He said that he's not good enough for me and that I could do so much better.

I told him that he was talking bullshit and that we should take one day at a time. I told him that I love him, and he said that he loves me too but that didn't change the fact that we should break up.

This morning when we spoke, he seemed less sure. He said that he didn't know what he wanted. We talked things through and he said that he didn't really want to break up with me, and he apologised for upsetting me.

I really do love him, and I don't want to lose him—ever. He is so sweet and kind, beautiful, handsome, and cute. He's all that matters to me. I couldn't cope without him. I live for seeing him.

X

24 September

Dear Diary,

We went out last night. It wasn't a bad night. When we got back to his place, we had sex three times!

But then he started again. He said, out of the blue, if I tell you something do you promise not to get upset? Then he said that he thought that we should break up. Again. I asked him what his reasons were this time and he said there was no reason. I burst into tears and tried to explain how much I love him and that I couldn't cope without him. He just kept saying "stop crying, if you love me, you'll stop crying".

He said that he didn't want to hurt me and that he loved me. Then he got passionate again and I took this as a sign that he had changed his mind, but when I asked him he said that nothing had changed. I got really angry and called him a fucking bastard. That didn't go down too well.

I couldn't stop crying. He said that he thought I was stronger than that, and I told him that I had never been strong. He said that I would cope without him and that it wasn't the end of the world. He said that we were bound to break up eventually so we might as well break up now.

He said that I make him feel second best.

I'm seeing him tonight to try and salvage something. It seems silly to end it now just when we're getting so close both mentally and physically.

Why break up when we care so much for each other?

X

25 September

Dear Diary,

When I saw him last night, he apologised and said that he didn't want to break up with me. He said that he just gets into these foul moods where he doesn't care about anyone or anything. He said that he still loves me.

We went out for a few drinks, and everything was fine, then he suddenly said "that's it, we're finished".

He thought that I was looking at another man.

He stormed out and I followed him back to his place. I tried to explain that I hadn't been looking at anyone, but he just wouldn't listen. He was incredibly angry. He said that no one had ever loved him so why should I? I was tempted to collect my things and go home but I didn't want to leave with the way things were. I didn't want to risk losing him. So I stayed.

Eventually he believed me when I said that I loved him and that I hadn't been— that I would never—look at anyone else. At least, I think that he believed me.

He says that he really loves me, even though it may not seem like it, and that he was just being stupid. But I'm worried that he will make a habit of these silly arguments. I don't think that I could cope with that. But I know that I couldn't live without him. I love him.

The rest of the evening was bliss. No sex though—which half-disappointed me, half-relieved me.

X

1 October

Dear Diary,

We have spent the last few days together. They were great, we had a really good time talking and messing about. We made love twice and I think we actually got it right—there were no arguments anyway! We even decided that we should move in together. We want a place in town so I can be near school—I'm nearly finished now, finally! I know my parents won't approve but we want to make a go of our relationship. We have become so close, and not just physically. We might even get engaged!

I want to be with him forever. I hope he realises just how much I love him. Being without him is inconceivable, I would rather die.

X

18 October

Dear Diary,

We've found a flat in town! God knows if we can afford it or even if it's a good idea moving in with him. My parents are furious, and I hate upsetting them, but it's my life and there's nothing they can do to stop me.

He's getting stressed out because we are barely seeing each other: I'm at school, he's had extra shifts at work—great for our deposit but not so great for our love-life. One minute he's saying that he loves me more than anything and that he can't wait for us to move in together and the next he's saying he's bored of us…I'm a little bit worried.

X

23 October

Dear Diary,

My period is three weeks late. He persuaded me to do a pregnancy test. I'm pregnant.

We are both confused and have mixed emotions. He says that he loves me and that he will stand by me. He says that he has no intention of leaving me.

Neither of us really know how to feel about this. I'm petrified about my parents' reaction and about what will happen to me—to us. I told him that a baby could ruin things, but he said it could bring us closer together.

I'm not sure that I want this. I'm too young. I haven't even finished school. But I can't have an abortion—I couldn't live with myself if I did that. And anyhow, he said that he'd leave me if I did.

I feel very confused.

X

2 December

Dear Diary,

Today has been the worst day of my life. The person I love more than anything in the world says he is leaving me and his unborn child over a simple misunderstanding.

I love him more than words can express, and I am glad that I'm having his baby, but I'm worried too. Today I tried to express my fears and worries about having a baby and being a mother, but I failed, and now he says we are finished.

I'm scared. I'm frightened that I won't cope, that I'll do something wrong. Mum and Dad still aren't speaking to me so I can't turn to them for support and advice. I suppose I've been focusing on the negatives. He thought that I was seriously considering an abortion as an option. I would never do that, and he should know that. I want this baby now more than ever. I know it will be hard—especially if I don't have him—and I know that me having this baby will upset a lot of people, but my mind is made up. I just need his support and his understanding. But he won't listen. He says that he's leaving me.

Living with him over these past few months has been bliss. We have had our ups and downs, but it's made me realise how much I really love him and need him. I never want to be without him. But he was so cruel to me this evening. Very cruel. I can hardly bear to write it down. He wished that he had never set eyes on me and that he had left me when he had had the chance. He said that I was cold and selfish and useless. He wished me and the baby dead.

I don't want to remember that. Instead I want to remember how it feels to be loved by him, to be held in his arms, to see his beautiful smile. I want to remember talking about our future, our plans as a family, about how much we love each other.

I suppose I should hate him for all the pain that he's putting me through, but I can't. I love him so much and it scares me to think of being without him. He doesn't want to be near me, and he says that he is leaving in the morning. Most of his things are already packed. I really think he hates me. I can't bear it. I keep hoping that he will want me again and that he'll stay, but I guess I'm being stupid. I just wanted to talk to him about my fears. I wanted him to hold me and to tell me that everything would be alright, for him to tell me that he loves me, and that we would be fine. Instead I got the prospect of being a single parent. And I *am*

having this baby. Selfish of me maybe, but at least I will have a part of him that I can love and look after.

Why won't he listen to me? I can't even talk to him to explain, to make him understand. It seems that the more I try to tell him how I feel about him and the baby, the more he hates me. I just can't bear it anymore. All I want is to be with him. Always. I want to remember all the good times—the laughter, the dancing, the kisses—not this. I want to remember how special he makes me feel. And I want our baby to know what a wonderful person he is. I love him so much.

Please don't let him leave me. I don't know what I'd do without him.

X

The Wife

It was no use. She still could not sleep. Her mind was in turmoil, re-visiting past events, and over-thinking everything she had ever said or done.

Her relationship with her husband was turbulent, it had been from the very beginning. They had been so young, not much more than children really. She had been a passionate but quiet and impressionable teenager who thought life was a romance novel; whilst he had been a surly and aggressive youth, but somehow at one and the same time sweet and sensitive. She could barely remember their early life together; it seemed a lifetime ago. She could only vaguely recall numerous arguments. Maybe they had simply enjoyed the drama or maybe they had both been too young and too scared at the prospect of adulthood and all its responsibilities.

Her memory of their early life may have been unreliable, but she could remember their move to be closer to his family—to have the support of his parents and a better paid, steady job. It was a move that had filled her with apprehension and anxiety: she had so wanted to rebuild the bridges with her own parents and to finish her schooling, but he had persuaded her that this would be better for them and for the baby, and so she had acquiesced.

The move had marked a change in their relationship. She felt all the more isolated while he reverted back to being a little boy around his parents and young, free, and single at all other times. He began meeting up with old friends—single friends—and spent most of his spare time socialising with them, crawling home in the small hours worse for wear from drink. She said nothing of course. How could she? It was his home, his turf, and she didn't want his parents to hear them

arguing. And in part it was also because she was concentrating on the new life growing within her, focusing on the baby that would be hers to love and in turn would love her unconditionally. She could endure his ignoring her, and she would endure his drinking and his rowdy friends. She would endure living with his parents—for now. A change was coming over her: she no longer needed him, she had this baby and that was all that mattered now.

Thoughts

Remember.

Remember when.

Remember when we were young, with no real worries or responsibilities.

Remember how eager we were to leave childhood behind. We couldn't wait to be all grown up, we thought life would be easier.

We played out our youth like a cheap soap opera. We had our own soundtrack, a song to reflect and enhance our every emotion.

Remember how easy it was to say "I love you".

We rushed through our youth, impatient for adulthood.

We should have lingered awhile.

III
Saving the Past

The Girl

16 July

Dear Diary,

On the 2 July, I gave birth to a beautiful, healthy baby girl. Things are, on the whole, perfect—except that we are still living with his parents, something I'm not happy about. Living with them may be helping us financially, and I know they are trying to help, but it feels like they're always interfering and criticising how I do things.

I still really miss Mum and Dad. I wish they would meet their granddaughter. I thought he would understand how I'm feeling, how lonely I am, but I don't think he does. Also, since we moved in with his parents, he's shown sides of himself that I really don't like or recognise; and he spends as little time as possible with me. And whereas he started off as a doting dad he doesn't seem interested anymore and he spends less and less time with his daughter.

But I'm sure things will get back to normal once we have our own place again. At least, I have my baby.

X

The Wife

When her baby was born, all three of them had found themselves growing up together. The child saw and heard everything, even what was left unsaid. She liked to think that her daughter had been too little to understand all the arguments, too little to be affected by her mother's tears. But children should never be underestimated.

In truth, she remembered very little of her daughter's first few weeks of life, but she did remember that when she had first held that tiny, precious bundle in her arms, her first thought had been that it would be better if the baby died now before she had the chance to become too attached to her and before this perfect creature became spoiled and sullied by life.

She had felt overwhelmed and dazed. Lost. But these feelings were only for the merest fraction of a second. Those thoughts and those emotions were fleeting; and as she gazed at the little baby nestled to her breast something had clicked into place. From that instant, all her energy, love and attention went to her daughter. Every waking moment was devoted to her child, and she loved her ferociously, protected her even more so, and constantly pushed her to achieve— to be all she could be and so much more. In short, to be better than her.

And now her daughter, her very reason for existence, was all grown up and no longer needed or wanted her, or so it seemed. The time had gone so quickly— in a heartbeat, the blink of an eye. She was out in the big, bad world, happy not to be at home where she had lived under the misguided belief that she had been unwanted—a mistake. Their daughter felt that she was the cause of her father's sadness and anger, and the reason for her mother's role as a martyr. For her, anywhere was better than home.

*

She could remember so little of her child and it made no sense that this was so. It frightened her. She wanted to remember it all, every single precious moment. But when she tried it was not the happy times that floated to the surface.

She remembers.

She remembers lying huddled on the couch, curled up in a protective ball as she rocked herself backwards and forwards. Her face was swollen and red from a long night of crying. Her teenage daughter had long since gone to bed, she knew that she could not be of any help—she didn't know how to calm a grown woman who was crying like a small child and threatening to commit suicide. So, she had sat alone. Every now and then she would mutter a few incoherent words before being pulled back into her web of hysteria, unaware that her daughter was alone and afraid too.

Time passed. She became exhausted by her emotions and slept a disturbed sleep where her dreams were filled with her worst fears: the truth that she had chosen long-since not to believe.

It had been well past midnight before her husband returned home. She thought that she would have got used to it by now, the nightly and daily disappearances, the hushed phone-calls, and the texts that she was not allowed to see. It was not the first time that something like this had happened, but

somehow it seemed far worse. Maybe she had not been able to cope because she had been ill at the time, or maybe it was because this time it seemed more real. Whatever the reason, she was scared. Her whole world seemed to be crumbling around her. Deep in her heart she had known what was going on, but she had refused to acknowledge the truth, because she had known that if she did, she would risk losing everything.

At the familiar sound of her husband's car pulling up outside the house, she rose quickly to her feet and almost ran to meet him at the door with the blind faithfulness and devotion of an old family dog. He pushed her roughly aside and headed straight for the drinks cabinet and poured himself a large whisky.

'What are you still doing up?' he asked angrily. 'Checking up on me? I'm not your baby, it's not my bedtime yet.'

She leant forward and attempted to kiss his cheek, but he turned abruptly away, disgust written on his face.

'Was the film good? I'd like to see it; you'll have to tell me all about it. It's been so long since we've been anywhere together—' she simpered.

'Then go and see it with him!' he interrupted. 'You can have that little pansy as your toy boy. All I ever hear from you is that you're discontented. Moan, moan, moan! Always asking me questions—where are you going? When will you be back? Who was that on the phone? You make me sick! If you're that discontented, then why don't you leave!'

'You know I'll never be discontented with you,' she pleaded. 'It's me that loves you, not her.'

'Don't start all that emotional blackmail again! I told you, we are just good friends,' he responded angrily.

'But you see her so often!' She found it hard to hold back the tears. 'You're hardly ever at home anymore and when you are you lock yourself away in a room and won't let me come in.'

'I get on well with her, I enjoy her company. We have got a lot in common. Plus, she doesn't whine and moan like you.'

'Please don't leave me! I don't want you to leave me,' she begged. 'I couldn't cope without you. I'll be a better wife, I promise, I—'

Her speech was cut short as hysteria welled up and threatened to overwhelm her.

'For God's sake, stop grizzling! I'm sick to death of your double standards. Get up the fucking stairs and go to bed! Go on! Get out of my sight!' he screamed, his sallow face contorting with ugly anger.

Sitting on the edge of her bed, their daughter sat listening to their raised voices, trying to control her rage and her fear which were almost consuming her. If only she knew what to do, but the situation was both beyond her understanding and her ability. She knew it was their problem, not hers, but whenever her mother cried it almost broke her heart and she felt that she had to intervene. As the voices grew louder, she could hold back no longer, and she rushed blindly down the stairs. She paused as she entered the room, shaking, unsure how to proceed, of what to say or do.

'Didn't I tell you to shut up and get upstairs!' he yelled. Then he noticed his daughter standing in the doorway.

'I suppose this is all for her benefit,' he growled, pointing to their daughter. 'I don't know why I bothered coming home.'

'Oh? And where would you have gone?' their daughter asked shakily, scared of her father's reaction. 'To your whore I suppose!'

'Don't talk to your father like that,' her mother spoke hurriedly. Her daughter wondered who she was trying to defend: them or him. Her husband turned and looked at her, a sneering smile playing on his lips.

'And what do you care, woman? You wanted her to come down and interfere, didn't you? That's why you started to whinge!' His voice rose to a crescendo.

'Don't talk to my mum like that!' their daughter cried bursting into tears. All the hatred and sadness she had locked up inside for all those years came out all at once. 'You don't give a damn about her! About us! You've never cared! All you care about is yourself and that bitch! I hate you!'

He grabbed his daughter by the shoulders. He shook her violently and slammed her into the wall. He pulled at her ears, her hair, scratched her face.

And all the while she had looked on. She had said nothing, done nothing to help her daughter. His face had become unrecognisable, his eyes were bulging and bloodshot, saliva trickled down his chin.

She had screamed, her precious daughter had screamed. She remembered every word, every action.

'Get your filthy hands off me! I hate you! I hate you both!'

'Don't you dare—' he slammed her head against the wall to emphasise his words, '—ever speak to me like that again you little slag! You're the bitch not her, you hear?'

'Bastard! You touch me one more time and I'll call the police!'

Once more, that sneering grin had played on his lips. He raised his hand above his head, and it came crashing down on the side of his daughter's face. Finally, she found her voice and began to shout weakly, pleading for her daughter.

'Please…stop!' she cried.

'She asked for it, the slut,' and he had flung her roughly away, discarding her like a used tissue. She staggered shakily over to the couch.

There was an interminable silence broken only by their daughter's stifled sobs. Then she turned to her husband, touched his arm tentatively and asked, 'Do you want a coffee, darling?'

'No. I don't want to be anywhere near *her*,' he said, jerking his head in his daughter's direction. 'She's always interfering. The little bitch has no consideration for you. She's a disappointment to me. I thought she knew better than to upset you, to fill your head with nonsense. She owes me an apology.'

He stormed out of the room and, obediently, she had followed him. Their daughter had remained on the couch, confused and shaken by her mother's dismissal and betrayal. She felt alone. Small. She rose and went quickly upstairs to the relative safety of her bedroom, pausing only to listen to the muffled voice behind her parents' closed door.

'She had no right to talk to me like that. She deserved what she got. I don't like to see you upset…I told you about her, I am very fond of her, but she doesn't feel the same way. I suppose I have got to lose the only real friend I've got because of your childish jealousy. I've lost too many friends that way…Jesus Christ! Will you stop looking at me like that!'

Time had passed. The sordid incident appeared to be forgotten by all. But she remembered, and so did their daughter. Things gradually had returned to their normal routine: hidden texts, mysterious phone calls, daily and nightly disappearances.

*

She lay huddled on the couch, remembering, curled up in a protective ball as she rocked herself backwards and forwards, her face red and swollen from crying. Her daughter had left home. She had no one now. So, she waited alone, lost in her private world of hysteria. Waiting.

Thoughts

I look at my child and it seems that she changes with every heartbeat. And I am scared. Scared for her and scared for me.

Where did the time go? How could I have missed the change from child to youth, from youth to adult?

She is slipping away from me, and she is taking with her my very sense of being, my sense of worth, my heart, and my soul. There is so much that I wanted to say to her, to share with her. So many adventures missed. So many regrets.

I wanted her to stay little, to stay perfect and pure. Why did she race to adulthood? I never gave her my permission to do so. Had she asked I would have said no, I would have explained that it would lead to nothing but pain and worry and disappointment and heartache. Far better to stay little and good. That way I could keep her safe.

But I am losing her. Correction: I have lost her. And I am so scared.

The Wife

Sleep was still keeping her awake. Rummaging through the oak dresser she found what she was looking for: her box of keepsakes and old photographs, and at the very bottom, her wedding album. She turned on the table lamp, curled up on the couch once more, and began to leaf through the album.

Her wedding day. What a day that had been. She had wrongly assumed that her parents would be pleased that she was marrying the father of her child, but no, they had been disappointed as usual. And there was of course disappointment for her too as there would be no dream church wedding, it was going to be low-key and lack-lustre—rather like the proposal. A proposal she had quickly accepted, spreading the good news immediately before he had time to change his mind.

She had tried to make the best of things and had asked her mother—correction, she had pleaded with her mother—to help choose her wedding dress. Nothing too fancy, they were only marrying in a registry office after all. She may have been denied a lavish church wedding, but she did have her heart set on a

gorgeous dress: a silk sheath with embroidery and sequins on the bust, simple yet elegant. But her mother had said no. It soon became apparent that the parents of the bride were not prepared to help, advise, or finance any aspect of their only child's wedding. So she had to make-do with a cream dress (a little too small) from a charity shop, and the groom had borrowed a suit from a friend. But the happy couple had hired a photographer and managed to scrape together enough money to buy some of the photographs. And if the photographs were anything to go by, the day had not been a complete disaster. Yes, there had been a definite division between the groom's side of the family and the brides (and had it really been necessary for her mother to wear black?). But the happy couple certainly looked happy, blissful even. In every photograph, the groom looked proud standing next to his shy, smiling bride. She remembered how her new husband had had her in a fit of giggles when the photographer had told him to cup her chin in his hand and gaze adoringly into his bride's eyes. That definitely had been the wrong time for him to say something silly and inappropriate, and as a result the photo was awful as they both had been laughing so much. Yet they had chosen to buy that photo in particular because they had been so happy in that moment, and it showed. A single moment of happiness preserved forever.

Their daughter had only been six years old at the time and she had looked adorable. She had hoped to get her a pretty flower girls dress, all frills and lace, but had to make do with what they could afford. But it hadn't mattered, she still had looked beautiful, and the photograph of the three of them—doting Dad, his arm draped protectively around his daughter's shoulder, smiling at each other with such unconditional love; the bride looking on, her eyes gazing devotedly at her new husband—was a favourite. They had looked so content. A perfect family.

The wedding day had not been perfect: no church service, no dress, no reception, and no honeymoon. Still. It didn't really matter. That is what she told herself as she sat curled up on the couch. Marriage should not be about material things. It was the vows that mattered. It was their promise to love, cherish, and honour each other "till death do us part".

The Lover

She waits nervously outside her local pub. He was supposed to have been here ten minutes ago. She pulls her scarf higher around her neck to keep out the chill, autumnal evening breeze. She ponders: *Stay a few more minutes or leave*

with at least a little pride intact? She decides on the latter. It's probably for the best that he didn't show. What on earth was she thinking, agreeing to meet him? Why would someone as gorgeous and sexy as him want anything to do with her?

She begins her walk home, strangely pleased that the world is back in balance: she is alone, unwanted, foolish, and he is unattainable. Then she sees him in her peripheral vision, running towards their rendezvous point; an intensity and a panic showing clearly on his face. She pauses and hesitates briefly before picking up her pace to retrace her steps and follow him.

Outside the pub again her panic is almost overwhelming: he is not there. Was she mistaken? Maybe he wasn't going to meet her after all. Then the door opens, and he is there.

'I thought you'd be gone,' he says breathlessly. 'I was looking for you inside.'

'No. I was just running a little late,' she responds.

A lie, but she doesn't want to appear too eager, too desperate.

'Come in for a drink,' he says smiling. 'My treat.'

'No, I can't. I'm sorry, it's too public. Someone might see us, put two and two together and come up with five,' she laughs nervously.

'What a love story,' he murmurs, a smile playing on his lips. 'All the getting ready, and then nothing happens.'

He moves closer to her until they are almost touching, before continuing.

'We have a connection, so much in common—the moon, the stars!' He glances heavenwards and laughs. She is struck again by that beautiful, boyish smile, by his eyes that seem to be able to look into her very soul.

'And history, travel,' he pauses. 'It's not just physical for me—although I'd take a one-night stand.'

He leans in for a kiss, but with that last comment he has broken the spell and she pulls away from him despite every fibre of her being wanting him, needing him.

He continues unabashed and determined.

'We could run away together. My family would never speak to me again and I'd be disappointing a lot of people.' Another pause. 'And you've got your family to think about.'

She sighs and leans into his shoulder. He holds her in his arms and murmurs his next words gently but with genuine confusion.

'I'd love to scan your head. I don't know what to make of you.'

He holds her close and she feels like she has come home. She stands on tiptoe and gently kisses his cheek, but he suddenly pulls away, obviously frustrated.

'You think it's wrong, me being here, saying how I feel—but you're doing the same thing! What's the difference?' His tone has changed now. He is irritable and angry. 'I don't understand you!'

He takes a few deep breaths, and the moment passes. He speaks again, but he is calmer now.

'I want you. You want me. Why not? So, let me know when you're ready, when you're free,' he gazes into her eyes as if she is all that matters to him. 'And don't stop texting me—I like it. It's always good to hear from you. When you're ready, we can meet for coffee. Let me know?'

Can she hear pleading in his voice? They hug each other but it is over all too soon. As he leaves, he turns and says urgently—as if he can read her mind—

'Try to stay away from negative thoughts!'

And he is gone.

The Woman

What did you expect when you arranged for us to meet?
I don't know.
You know I like you…
We can't. My family.
Forget about them for once. Live in the moment.
My moments should be with them.
We could be so good together if things were different, if we'd have met before.
That's a lot of ifs.
I dream about you.
Don't.
Will I see you again?
I don't know. Maybe. I hope.

Thoughts

What is this obsession with our past, with living in our memories, and constantly going over prior events? Why do we choose the "what ifs" and "if only" when we can have the here and now? Is it because our present is too unbearable, too painful, and our future too uncertain? Is that why we choose the

relative safety of our memories? Or are we remembering so that we can begin to forget.

The Woman

You promised me some dirty photos.
Soon.
Here are some for you.
You are one gorgeous man. I can't wait to be with you.
What are you sending me? I want to be ready. I can't even write, that's how horny I am.
I'll send something later.
Will you get fucked tonight thinking of my cock inside you?
Maybe. I want it to be you inside me.

Thoughts

My fantasy. To spend a few days with you, no time constraints. To go out together. To make love whenever we want: sensual and romantic, hardcore and kinky. Whatever we like. To fall asleep next to you and wake up with you.

Dream on baby. It will never happen.

The Wife

He is finally home, tired from work, surly from drink, and hungry. But she is hungry too. She wants him, she needs him. She needs to feel something even if just for a short while, she needs to pretend that everything is ok—that everything will be ok. She follows him upstairs to the bedroom and climbs onto his lap, straddling him, their naked skin hot against each other. This is when he is truly hers, this is their time of true connection. Their lips find each other's, and they kiss passionately as his hands caress her arching back. Her hands are firmly gripping his strong shoulders and she moves her hips backwards and forwards rhythmically until he begins to get hard.

His lips travel down to her full breasts, and he sucks and kisses her nipples, making her sigh with pleasure. Then his hand begins to travel downwards until his fingers are inside her. She is moist and welcoming. He moves gently at first but as their passion increases, he quickens, and with each thrust of his hand she screams in sheer ecstasy. Removing his hand, he now thrusts himself deep inside

her. He is hard, firm, powerful. She arches her back in response and with both hands he slaps her buttocks. With each slap, she screams "yes" and begs him to hit her harder, to move deeper, faster; to reach that point where pleasure meets pain. She screams again. Fuck! Yes baby! Yes baby! He moves faster and faster until she comes with a satisfied sigh.

He throws her onto her back. It is his turn now. His lips find her soft and wet, his tongue tastes her sweetness as he licks her gently, making her moan once more. Then he is inside her again. She catches her breath with the force of his passion. She kisses him and grabs at his back, his chest, his buttocks; her nails scratching and tearing at his flesh as he pushes into her, crushing her body to his chest. She screams in pain, a pain that is combined with sweet rapture and for a brief moment he rises above her and moves more gently before increasing the tempo once more. She holds his face in her two hands and their lips touch briefly—a butterfly kiss—before he pulls away. She clings to his strong forearms, watching his chest arching gracefully but strongly above her, watching as his penis moves in and out of her, listening to the sounds of his pleasure as he climaxes.

He falls onto her, entirely spent. She runs her fingers through his hair and gently brushes his cheek with her fingertips before he rolls onto his side and falls into a deep sleep, leaving her alone once more.

Thoughts

I am mesmerised by the photograph. He is perfection. A god come to life. Every inch of his muscled, tanned body is perfect: his firm biceps, his taut stomach, his impressive penis. I want to hold him again, to touch him, to feel for one last time the warmth of his skin on mine and his probing lips against my own.

I want to meld my body to his, for us to become one. To become a two headed, four-legged monster. I want to feel him inside me.

But is he real? He is too perfect. Too good to be true. Why would he want me? Do I really know him? Have I really touched him, caressed him, kissed him? It seems like a dream. A fantasy.

Another photograph. The woman looks vaguely familiar. She is almost beautiful. Her piercing blue eyes lock onto mine accusingly. Her moist red lips are partially open, ready to devour the tumescent penis which she grips firmly in one hand. She is claiming ownership like a feral cat pissing on a tree.

Put the photos away. It's too much. I shouldn't torment myself with what can never be. I should leave the past in the past. I need to learn to forget.

The Girl

25 October

Dear Diary,

I don't know what to do. I thought that everything was ok. Things have been great between us for a long time now. Married four years, we even have our own place. He works full-time so we have no money worries. And I love being a full-time mum, I always have.

But there's someone else.

He said why shouldn't someone have more than one partner, and have feelings for more than one person? He said that there isn't just that one special person out there waiting for us—there are many. He said why shouldn't we grab happiness when and where we can. He says that life is too short not to live in the moment. I don't think it's love. But it seems special—it's that need to be wanted.

I am so confused.

X

The Woman

We're having a telepathic affair. Send me a picture. I'm curious if you'll play the game.

You have no morals.

Please. I don't want to sound perverted, but I want pictures. I liked seeing your decolletage the other day. First time I've seen you exposed. Very nice.

Maybe I need to keep what's left of my dignity.

Don't.

I get the feeling that I'm more interested in you than you are in me.

Not at all, but I don't know what this game is. You're my friend but I want you sexually too, but I don't think you are ok with that. My wife knows. We have no secrets. She's ok with this. So, I suppose it's your move.

I don't know. I want you as a friend and more too. It's all so complicated. I shouldn't even be thinking of you let alone contacting you. Sometimes I wish that I had never met you.

IV
Self-Destruct

The Lover

She met him again in the pub. It was a hot and sultry summer's afternoon and it had taken a lot of self-persuasion to get her there. He had bought her a glass of wine and she had cradled it nervously as they chatted, sharing stories of their youth, getting to know each other better.

Drinks finished; he had decided that they should go for a walk. All she wanted to do was to hold his hand, to feel his skin on hers, but every time her hand had brushed his, he had pulled away. Maybe she had been reading the signals wrong.

They sat side by side on a bench in a quiet spot in the park. At first, the conversation continued, but it was more philosophical now: the meaning of life, what is happiness, what exactly is love? They were sitting so close together that she could feel the heat emanating from his body. He leaned in and they kissed, and as their lips touched, he moved her hand onto his lap. He was large and firm. Now it was her turn to pull away, she felt confused and unsure. He appeared neither offended nor upset by her response. He gazed into her eyes and gently brushed her hair away from her face before leaning in for another kiss.

'I should go,' she said.

He followed her as she walked away and then grabbed her, pulling her back into him until she fitted perfectly into the curves of his strong body. He twisted her hair in his hand, revealing her neck and kissed her passionately as his free hand moved up to caress her breasts. Her body arched and shivered in response to his touch.

'I should go,' she repeated, torn between physical desire and common sense.

Reluctantly he released her. She turned and kissed him before quickly walking away, her heart racing. The further she walked from him, the sadder she felt.

The Woman

That picture was yummy.

Thanks. How many other women send you naughty pictures?

Not so many.

In that case, you won't be needing anymore from me…you owe me a naughty picture now by the way, so make sure don't forget! And I hope you realise what you mean to me. It's breaking my heart not seeing you. I want to be able to spend time with you like we did that afternoon in the summer, do you remember? I want to talk and feel your skin on mine, I want to feel you inside me too. I worry that you don't feel the same. It drives me crazy.

I do feel the same.

*

Hi. I'm free Wednesday if you want to get together.

You have a death wish. I'll think about it.

I have my friend's house for an hour. I could pick you up and drop you back happy and refreshed.

I don't know. I don't want to be used.

You are not used.

I don't know if this is a good idea.

It's a great idea. Anyway. I won't put pressure on you.

I want to but it's wrong.

Stop over-thinking everything.

We shouldn't. It's not right.

I just want a safe place so we can have coffee. So I can take care of you.

I don't know.

I'll call you in the morning. Like I said, no pressure.

*

Hey.

Hey. How's things?

Good. It's all sorted for tomorrow. How's your spirit?

Same as usual.

Insecure, questionable, doubtful?

50

Of course. I'm consistent if nothing else. Why do you like me?

I like you because we have things in common. Because we have a connection. You are my friend. And you're weird!

But your wife…

Stop over-thinking and live in the moment! We've been like this for what? A year? She'd be jealous if you loved me not if we have sex. Let me play.

I'm not having sex with you.

Love me then.

The Lover

He drove her to his friend's house, chatting nervously all the way and she wondered what the hell she was doing.

Once inside the unassuming terrace house which his friend had—for some unknown reason—agreed to lend them for their sordid assignation, they headed for the kitchen.

'A drink?' he offered. 'Tea? Coffee?'

'Is that what you say to all the other women that you bring here?' she responded, half in jest, throwing her bag on the floor and leaning nervously against the countertop. This doesn't feel right to her, she is already feeling used and dirty before anything has even happened.

'Why do you always say things like that to me?' he said, his face is crestfallen, and he is obviously hurt by her comment. 'You always have to make me feel stupid and wrong.'

'Sorry,' she mumbled, wishing that she could take back her words.

After a brief and awkward silence, he sat down on a chair at the kitchen table and beckoned her over. She sat opposite him, and he leant forward to gently kiss her. Then lifted her to her feet and, kissing and caressing her all the while, he attempted to manoeuvre her to the couch. But she had not been able to shake her nervousness and she stopped every now and then, playing for time.

'Stop dragging your feet,' he scolded playfully.

Finally, they reached the couch, and she found herself lying on her back, his strong hands searching, reaching inside her clothing, and she realised once again, that she cannot do this.

'I'm not going to have sex with you,' she said abruptly, pushing herself—and him—into an upright position.

'Why not?' he responded, unsurprised, settling himself comfortably on the couch beside her.

'It's wrong,' she said firmly.

'Ah here!' he sighed, obviously frustrated. He put his arms around her and held her close. 'I'm not going to force you,' he murmured, kissing the top of her head.

As they walked back to his car she had asked if she would see him again, but he had just smiled enigmatically, shrugging his broad shoulders. Suddenly she had wanted to rewind, to go back in time, back to the couch: she should have slept with him, she doesn't want to lose him.

'You're not going to get all romantic on me and cry, are you?' he asked noticing the change that has come over her.

'No!' she replied, attempting to pull herself together.

He turned to unlock the car but before he can open the door, she called his name and as he turned to her, she reached up and kissed him passionately.

'What was that for?' He is surprised but pleased.

'Because I wanted to,' she whispered.

'Don't tell me that you love me?' he mocks, but behind the mocking tone there is a degree of seriousness.

'No!' she responded, feigning contempt. Lying.

'OK,' he paused. 'Are you coming?'

'No. I think I'll walk. You never know who might see us,' she said quietly.

He smiled sadly as he replied, 'I don't care who sees us.'

The Woman

How are you?

Good. Enjoying a romantic evening with my wife. I'm focusing on my marriage. *You are a self-obsessed, egotistical bastard! I can't believe I fell for your bullshit! You know I have feelings for you and you're obviously just using me! I hope you're proud of yourself.*

What the fuck? What is wrong with you?

It doesn't matter.

Then why did you send that text if it doesn't matter?

I'm just fed up with being taken for granted by everyone. I'm feeling sorry for myself that's all. Like I said, it doesn't matter.

Ok. What are you expecting me to say?

Nothing.

*

Sorry I texted you yesterday when you were with your wife. I get that your marriage is your priority, I just feel a bit hurt. It's stupid of me, I know.
What do you want? Let me understand please.
I want you. But I can't.
I told you that she knows everything.
And she's not happy about it.
And…
She's texted me, told me to back off.
Ok. I'm a married man and you know that.
I know…
And?
I don't know. But it's nice to feel wanted and liked even if you don't really feel that way.
Did I promise something?
No. You're just playing games and messing with my head.
What games? What the fuck?

*

Hey. How are you?
Not great. I don't feel wanted. Don't mind me, I'm still feeling sorry for myself.
Don't. I want you. You'll get more than you're asking for. That will help you sleep.
No reaction?
I don't know what to say.
A hint? I'll send you a dirty movie…
No thanks.
You are the most adventurous human being…
To be fair you don't really know me.
In what way?
In any way.

You're wrong. I tend to be good at reading people. You have to admit that I'm like a shot of adrenaline in your life.

And what am I to you?

Hmm, a good one. I think that is very much up to you.

That's a cop out. You haven't answered my question.

I have done everything so that you can be in my life. It's very much your choice now.

You're a bad influence.

For sure.

I'm nothing special.

You're very wrong. You can be anything that you want to be. You just need to feel that you are loved and wanted.

I believed that before…

What do you think of everything?

Think of what exactly?

Sometimes I feel that I need to spell everything out for you…me, her, you. Especially me.

I'm tempted. But I'm also scared. And I'm worried that I'm just a big joke to you.

First, you are not a joke. Second, I see the situation as beneficial for all of us. Why are you scared?

I'm scared of the consequences. And how can it be beneficial? It's fucked up. I feel like I'm in self-destruct mode.

I think you're in self-discovery mode.

I don't like this new me. She's too selfish.

You don't know that yet. Selfish? It's debateable. I think you'll get more self-esteem. I know what I want myself. I know that I would like to spend more time with you and do so many things. We just have to try not to overthink everything.

I know I regret overthinking when we were at your friend's house…

We wouldn't have had time anyway, I'm a long lover!

Do I make you laugh sometimes?

You do.

What do you think of her?

She doesn't like me. At best, she pities me.

She likes you…and yes, she pities you as well. I'm sure if she got to know you…you're very shy and quiet, maybe after a few drinks you'd be different!

I'm shy and quiet when I don't know people and when I'm waiting on an angry wife to beat me up for hitting on her husband, I'm not exactly full of confidence. As for drinking, I either fall asleep or dance.

No funny stuff?

Like?

Really? Like…people tend to be without inhibitions when drinking. Like there usually is some behaviour change.

I prefer to be sober so I can be in control.

I don't see you as the type in control. For some reason, I see you as sexually very submissive. Am I wrong? I'd love to be wrong. Is it ok to talk about this?

It's odd to talk about this.

I find it natural, but I'm a pervert!

I'm confident enough not to be submissive…unless that's what's wanted…

I find that incredibly attractive when a person switches between being submissive and being dominant. What do you think about doing it with a woman?

I wouldn't rule it out.

Perfect answer.

So, do you do this often? Am I just another in a long line of women? Am I nothing special to you?

What the fuck! No! This isn't casual.

Why me?

Because you need this, and we need this. I think…I mean, we have to spend some time together and see if everything clicks. It's not only sex from my side, I also think it's important to be friends. This will be good for all of us.

Say something.

I think it could be disastrous in so many ways.

Like?

Marriages ruined; feelings hurt…

My marriage? Definitely not. Feelings…I don't think so. We're fucked up anyway.

My feelings…

Your feelings…I don't think so. You're not losing anything, you're gaining loads.

You always mind-fuck me. I decide not to be influenced by you, but you always end up confusing me.

55

How am I confusing you?

I never really know where I stand...and I start off determined that we are just going to be friends, but you always get under my skin again...

It's simple. We are friends and we could be more, but no one says that it will work. It could be perfect, or it might not, but there's only one way to find out. Your advantage is that you dictate timewise.

Now you're making me laugh. Excellent hard sell. Maybe you should go into politics!

Never say never!

I think I need my beauty sleep. I shall say goodnight.

You see, your timeframe. Say something nice and wet and kinky before you go.

We're just friends remember? Maybe I'll dictate here too—you say something.

I would kiss you everywhere right now.

Goodnight.

You're killing your friend!

Goodnight.

V
The Madness of Love

The Woman

When you're, I don't know, looking at the stars, or listening to music, do you ever wonder what I'm doing?

Yes.

I can talk to you about things I can't with anyone else…can I still call you?

Yes.

I can meet you whenever you are free. We could spend a day together…if you want…let me know.

What would this day entail? And what happens after this day?

Use your imagination for details. After that? I don't really know. Do you?

I know I think that I better focus on something other than you.

You can't.

Oh yes I can.

At least, I know what I want.

I know what I want too.

What?

Time alone with you, even if you are messing with me.

I'm not messing with you. I'll see you soon. I'll give you that kiss.

Careful, I might hold you to that.

*

I've thought and I've thought. We could run away together, find a deserted island, live happily-ever-after…but that's not going to happen. My idea is logical. Pervy but logical. I know what I want. Can you get away? Do you miss me? Do you think about me?

Yes, I miss you and I think about you.

So meet me.

You know that it's not that easy.

What's the point? Phone calls and texts are not my style.

What is your style then?

59

Not lying. Not hiding my desires and my feelings. It's annoying to see you in that little cage of yours. It's all mind-fuckery…nothing else. I love being your friend, but I want more. So?

I love being your friend too, but my feelings are more than that and it's hard knowing that you really don't feel the same.

I don't have feelings for you? I do. I think that I've proved over the years that I have feelings for you, but sure…we might as well be pen-pals these days.

Tell me how you feel then.

What's the point?

Because I want to know. I have a few minutes to myself. Talk to me.

Again…why should I only be here when you have a few minutes to spare? At the end of the day what is the outcome? Meet up twice a year for an evening, for a few minutes?

Fine. You know how I feel. You know how to contact me if you change your mind.

You're wrecking my head. Change what? I can't fucking change anything. You're the only one.

You have a wife. She loves you.

True. But *I* didn't hide anything did I?

I know that. I want to be your friend yes, and I do I want more.

How?

Exactly.

Now you tell me. You're never allowed out to play and a few minutes here and there is surely not my style, but I did it because I was missing you, but I guess you didn't know how hard it was for me to arrange that.

I do know how hard that was. But I'm just never sure if I'm not just a diversion.

A what? From what?

From whatever is missing or wrong in your life.

Of course you're filling in some blanks in my life but I'm sure that I'm the same for you.

What did you mean before? When you said that I'm the only one?

You're the only one who can change the situation.

Glad I clarified that. For a second there, I thought you might have feelings for me.

Really? Do you need confirmation that badly?

Yes.

I have feelings for you and you are a very special person in my life. Happy?

No. I'm still sad.

What do you need to feel better?

I don't know.

Of course. So you. If someone wrote a book about our love, it would be called A Billion Words About Nothing.

For the record, for my part it wouldn't be about nothing. It would be about a connection. I have to go. Remember that I love you.

Love you too.

I will try and see you soon.

Maybe a dirty weekend?

You have a one-track mind. That's lust not love.

Forgive my impurity.

Forgiven.

The Lover

When she had first met him, it had been an instant connection, like it was always meant to be. It was destiny or fate. It wasn't just a physical attraction, it was a meeting of minds and it felt comfortable, and she felt safe. She had believed that she had found a kindred spirit. A soulmate.

The day that they finally gave into their emotions he had been so gentle and understanding—caressing her face and stroking her hair. She had felt so special, and she had not felt that way in such a very long time.

When she had tried to do the right thing and leave, he had stood behind her, his left arm around her shoulder and neck, and he had pulled her into him. She had felt his warmth and hardness against her, his lips on her neck and on her shoulder. And she had allowed him to guide her upstairs. He couldn't get her undressed quickly enough. He kissed her breasts and explored every inch of her body, and she, in turn, as her confidence and her lust grew, explored his. Her hands tangled in his greying hair, her tongue explored his mouth, and her fingers traced the tattoo on his right bicep before dropping to grasp his tumescent penis. And when she had said that she couldn't do this, that she couldn't have sex with him, that it wasn't right; he had held her close and they had lain entwined together, her head nestled in the crook of his left arm, his right arm encircling her body protectively. He had said that he wanted to stay like that forever, just the two of them. She turned her head and kissed his perfect lips and wished, not for the first time, that she could stop time and capture the moment forever.

The Woman

It was lovely seeing you yesterday.

Same.

Wish I could see you whenever I wanted.

But you can.

I have to sneak around...

Sneak anytime. She said you can call into to me for a one-to-one. With a condition though.

That she kills me afterwards?

No. That we tell her what we do. Kinky stuff. She wants photos.

Kinky and incriminating then...

No no no! Not our faces! I think it's a fair deal.

I don't know what to say. Maybe...

We both know what you're going to say.

Really? And what's that?

Yes yes yes! Or maybe, maybe, maybe...

A definite maybe...maybe. I want to say yes but...

I need to be inside you soon. I think we've done this too many times in our heads. Agreed?

Yes. But I'm scared. Pathetic, I know.

No, it's normal to be scared. But what are your fears?

I'm nothing special—you'll be disappointed.

But you are so wrong. You are very special to me and that's all that matters. And I don't have any expectations so I can't really be disappointed, can I?

No response? Did my lovely words send you to sleep?

No. I just wish you were here now.

No, I wish you were here now. Do you ever touch yourself thinking of me?

Yes.

Hmmm...me too. I'm always coming so hard thinking of you. Tell me, what do you imagine?

Just to feel your skin against mine, to feel you inside me...

I can't wait. What if you're disappointed? I'm nothing special either.

You are. Just being near you and I'm happy.

Imagine me in you. You'll be thrilled. Are you smiling now?

I am.

Do we have to be drunk for this to happen?

Why? Do you need beer goggles?

No! I just don't want you all shy.

Me? Shy? Never!

Yeah right! I was dreaming that at some stage you might transform into a kinky dominatrix, all leather and PVC, and you'll tie me to the bed.

I quite like to be spanked in case you're interested...

I knew that.

How?

Just a vibe. I was sure that you were submissive.

I'm not that submissive...I like to be on top as I'm being spanked...this is getting very awkward...

No no no. It's getting there and I love it. I love knowing what you're like. I was thinking more the spanking as foreplay, bending you over and making your ass red. What turns you on?

At the minute, you.

Only at the minute?

Always. Especially now.

I came so hard thinking of you the other day...I was going to show you, but I never got the chance...want to see?

Yes.

Are you alone?

Yes.

Touching yourself?

Maybe...

Are you wet? I want you so much right now. Can I see how wet you are?

I'm shy.

I know. Take a pussy selfie.

You'll have to wait for the real thing.

Now you're mind-fucking me.

I'll fuck you properly later.

Will you fuck me good?

I promise. I want you deep inside me.

I can do anything I want with you?

What do you have in mind?

Tie you up. Use you. But maybe not the first time.

Are you going to be gentle at first then?

We'll start softcore. Unless you want hardcore first.

We'll see.

Always an enigma!

That's me.

I want to kiss you again.

Me too.

It kills me not being able to touch you.

I know.

I'd love to be outdoors with you and do stuff. Will you eat me?

If you're very good, I might.

No, I'm very bad. Will you do that for me?

Maybe. There's plenty I will do, assuming we actually get together.

Assuming? We will.

Careful, I might hold you to that.

You don't have to. Whenever you want and whenever you are free. I'll have the house empty and the toys out.

I'm never free…

I don't have toys…

You'll have me.

I'll rip off all your clothes.

Tell me more.

And I'll lift your skirt and lick you and spank you and bite your lips…will you suck me off and look into my eyes when you're doing it?

I might. I'm definitely wet now.

I'd love to lick it now. Have it all over my face. Tell me how you touch yourself.

I touch and caress my breasts until my nipples are hard and firm, then I slowly move my hand lower and rub my pussy. I rub harder and slide my fingers inside me, imagining you inside me, wanting you inside me…

I'd love to be inside you now. Where would you have me come?

In me.

Want to make a baby?

What!

You'll rediscover yourself with me.

When?

Anytime you want and for as long as you wish.

Come to my place tomorrow, I have an hour free. It's not long I know, but I'm sure we could make good use of the time.

I'm not doing that. We need more than one hour even if how sexy you are is killing me.

I bet that we never get together...

We will. Should I let you sleep? After the mind-fuck?

Please try and meet me tomorrow.

You could come to mine.

Ok.

Night-night?

I guess, not that I'll be able to sleep now.

Shut your kinky mind and go to sleep. You'll need your energy for tomorrow.

Goodnight.

The Girl

30 October

Dear Diary,

We have been honest and upfront with each other and, believe it or not, I think that it has helped. Don't get me wrong, I'm not happy about what happened but at least it wasn't as bad as it could have been. It was just a few text messages, the occasional brief meeting.

It was only flirtation. Just touching. No actual sex.

But what if it had been more? What if it could be more? I want to know, I want to know everything, to know what could happen, what might be possible. That way maybe we can work through it properly and our relationship and our marriage can be saved. Guilt has been confessed, and hopefully that means it won't happen again. I want our family to stay together, I really do, but no one said it wouldn't—or couldn't—happen again.

Why would anyone in their right mind risk losing their family for a sordid fumble? If someone flirts with you, you should tell them where to go, not encourage them. You may be flattered but you're meant to value your relationship and not do anything that may jeopardise it.

We need to think about what we could lose. There won't be a second chance, I know that much for certain. It would be foolish to throw away what we have, to

risk being alone over this. I firmly believe that we can get through this. We have to.

X

17 November

Dear Diary,
He is still being so distant with me. Nothing I say or do seems to help. I told him that I love him still. Everything is meant to be forgiven but he still keeps pushing me away.
Mobile phones are being monitored; the telephone bill has been checked—it shows certain phone calls—incriminating phone calls. But he won't discuss it with me. He refuses to say anything or to tell me anything. I wish I knew what he was thinking.

X

30 November

Dear Diary,
The past few weeks have been hell. All I do is cry and when we do try to talk about things, we just end up shouting at each other. He barely talks to me, and he can't even look me in the eye let alone have any physical contact with me. I feel so sick, and our daughter is suffering too. She doesn't understand why we are always screaming at each other.
Today he announced out of the blue that he is moving back in with his parents and he said that we can both have whoever we want now.
I don't know what to do anymore.

X

19 December

Dear Diary,

I wish he knew how I felt, how much I love him. He's been gone for nearly three weeks now and it hasn't been easy. I still cry at night, but I have to be strong for my daughter as well as being strong for me. She's coping quite well as I can explain certain things to her and console her, but she's still so confused and angry.

Last weekend was lovely—he came home for a visit. He was more talkative, and he even gave me a hug. I didn't think that everything was miraculously ok or that he'd be home for Christmas, but it definitely was a step in the right direction. But everything seems to have gone wrong again. Rumours have been spread around town and he thinks that I'm responsible. Why would I spread rumours? Why would I jeopardise getting our family back together? I don't care about gossip, and neither should he. People were bound to find out that he's moved out. And as for what happened, as far as I'm concerned, it's in the past. That's all that should matter. Who cares what other people may think?

Why doesn't he want to come home? I'm afraid that the longer he stays away the harder it will be for him to return. Maybe he won't come back. Maybe he doesn't want to.

The sooner he's back the better, then things can go back to normal, back to how they used to be. We shouldn't be living in the past.

X

22 December

Dear Diary,

He's still staying at his parents' house. I don't know where I stand. I wish he loved me as much as I love him. I'm scared and I'm lonely. I feel so stupid.

Sometimes I think we still have a chance but maybe I'm just being naïve. I just want things back to how they used to be.

X

VI
Pièce De Résistance

The Woman

Hey look. I have something to tell you. I was with someone else yesterday. I'm sorry. I didn't mean to hurt you. It just happened. Friends still?

I am hurt. I meant it when I said I love you and that I wanted more. But yes, friends always. But I also hate you at the minute.

That's understandable.

I feel so stupid for caring about you. But at least I still have a friend I suppose.

You will always have a friend.

I still want you even though you're an arsehole. You may not have meant it when you said that you loved me, but I meant it, and not just in a platonic sense. I can't believe that yesterday while I was wishing I could have stayed with you, you were screwing someone else.

I don't know what to tell you.

Where I stand. How you feel about me.

I need a few days to figure it all out. It's weird right now. I literally don't know what to say.

That makes me feel even more like shit.

I'm sorry. But I don't want to lie to you.

Then don't. I love you. Meet me soon? I need to talk to you face to face.

Yes, sure. Any time you want.

Actually, no talk. Just fuck me. No more talk. We can talk later.

You only make an effort now?

At least, I'm not sleeping with other people. Next time I see you if you don't rip my clothes off be prepared to have yours ripped off instead.

Sorry, but as I said I need time if you don't mind. My life is weird enough right now and I'm trying to figure it out.

I'm sorry. But I feel jealous—I now have to compete with your wife and your girlfriend? Are you still going to see her?

I don't really know. It was just the one time…

Ok…do you still want me or are we really just friends now?

I can't answer questions that I don't have the answers for.

71

I'm trying to make more of an effort for you, to take the initiative. When can I come and see you?

I honestly don't know. I need more time, please.

Am I a problem now? Do you want me as a lover? A friend? Neither?

You come over; we chat. What's the point? You're constantly watching the clock all the time. Then after, when you're home, you text to give out, to say if only, what if. Am I right? I don't even know what to call what it is that we're doing.

No more complaining, I promise. No more ifs and buts.

What I'm saying is I need time to figure out everything in my life. I don't have any answers right now.

You're breaking my heart.

I don't want to break anything. Nothing will change between us; we can still meet up every now and then for a drink.

I want more than that. We're soulmates.

Well maybe in a parallel world we're soulmates, but in this one I'm a married man.

And I'm a woman who loves you and wants you. I'm fed up of missing out on life and of people taking me for granted. I'm coming over tomorrow.

Don't assume I'm free just because you find a window in your schedule. I'm trying to be really nice to you but it's the same thing over and over again. I can't see you at the minute, I need to spend time with my wife.

I'm coming over tomorrow.

Can't you fucking read?

The Girl

15 January

Dear Diary,

He came home. I told him that he couldn't just come and go as he pleased, that he had to make a decision one way or another. It did the trick and he's been trying ten times harder to make things work. Now I just have to try and do the same.

X

2 February

Dear Diary,

It's three in the morning and he's still not home. He stormed out because there were more text messages today: *I will always be there for you no matter what; I can't give you what you want; maybe we can still meet up; I'm married, I have too much to lose, sorry; I'm the one who's always there for you; can we meet; I'll try.*

He got incredibly angry when the messages were seen. Threatening. He trashed the house. He said nasty things to me and to our daughter. Then he stormed out. He's back now. He came home a few hours ago. He seems to have conveniently forgotten everything he said and did. I suppose he'll remember everything when he sobers up.

I don't know what to do. We had been doing so well. I must be very stupid.

I do love him, and I don't want him to leave. I can't bear the thought of being without him again, of being alone. But it's almost as lonely when he is here.

I guess I'll just have to wait and see what happens.

X

5 February

Dear Diary,

There has been more, shall we say, indiscretion.

I think that it all needs to be out in the open: the who, the why, the what. There's no point in denial anymore.

We need to work out what it is that is so wrong with our relationship that another person is so easily turned to. We need to be honest with each other, to share our feelings, to admit what has happened, and why it happened. We need to decide who and what we want. If we choose to stay together and try to work things out, then there can be no one else. But I'm too much of a coward to face the truth head on.

What I do know is that if there is any more cheating—even if it's just a text— then we are finished for good.

The Wife

She really was not sure if she could go through with it. Killing herself that is. The idea had been appealing for quite some time, but she did have concerns. She was worried as to what happened after the deed was done. It was ridiculous really; she had spent her entire life believing that when you died that was it. Game over. Now however, she kept on thinking of all the horrendous things that might be waiting for her. But it could not be much worse than what she had been through already, what she was going through now.

Her life had not been all that bad and plenty of people had had a great deal worse—they had more reason than her to commit suicide. And it was not as if there hadn't been people who had loved her and cared about her. Correction: people had used to love and care about her. Past tense.

She had had a relatively good childhood—just the one major glitch, but she did not like to dwell on that particular experience. All the bad things she had shut out anyway, remembering only fragments, bits and pieces. Her childhood was quite a shattered story. In truth, things had only been going from bad to worse in recent years. Her marriage had been going through a sticky patch for quite some time and she had not handled things well—and she still did not. Neither of them had helped the situation, she had been shutting him out since her pregnancy, and since her daughter's birth had focused solely on being a mother and putting all of her energy into that role. He, in response, had kept on disappearing for hours on end and when he returned home he was usually drunk and gave lame excuses for his absence. When their daughter was older, he sometimes came home with gifts for his wife and child—but she perceived the gifts as a sure sign of a guilty conscience as opposed to what they were in actuality—a simple peace offering, an apology. The situation was very upsetting for all involved, and their daughter, who was now old enough to finally understand some of what was going on in her parents' relationship, began to distance herself from them both but in particular from her father. She simply could not bear to be in the same room with him, especially when he had been drinking, and she always found a way to contradict him and to antagonise both him and the situation.

The disappearances had got worse and worse, he just could not bear to be at home. There were times when they only saw him at mealtimes. Their daughter didn't really care that much, she preferred it without him—it was calmer—but she could not endure seeing her mother so upset. She began to hate her father and to hate her home. Both mother and daughter were distressed, and

unbeknownst to either parent, their daughter began to spend all of her spare time trying to find out where her father went to and why, hoping that she could help things get back to normal. She had just wanted to help.

Eventually she did discover the truth. All those years of loyalty, devotion, and love. They had both taken each other for granted. The marriage was a sham. In the end, it had been relatively easy for her to find out about them, they had not been particularly discreet, and all of the excuses were so obviously lies. It was all bullshit. All she had had to do was to look through the diary, to rifle through drawers and cupboards, to check through the contents of bags and coat pockets, and to check phone messages. It had been quite easy as neither parent believed that their daughter would dare to go through their private belongings.

The things that she found made her stomach turn and had turned her world upside down. She found house keys (and not to the family home), presents, messages, and love letters. She had read the messages and love letters of course. It was sick. They can't have been in love like they proclaimed, just in lust. She felt it might have been easier for her to understand if it had been love. She had found that she could not just stand back idly and do nothing, to watch as the deceit continued, and so she had revealed her findings to them, so as to set the record straight. She had believed that she was helping. She believed that if only she had loved her father more and had been more understanding, if she had been a better daughter for her mother and achieved all that she had envisioned for her, then perhaps there would not have been any infidelity.

Despite his anger and the continuation of his disappearances, initially there was no confrontation between husband and wife. Her mother instead chose to adopt the role of the innocent, obedient, and faithful little housewife in the hope that all the trouble would simply disappear. Her daughter was confused, she didn't understand why her parents were not confronting the issue and trying to resolve it, and she really didn't understand her mother's stance as a martyr. Maybe she did love her father after all.

Eventually the tension became too much, and the confrontations occurred. They would lock themselves away for hours on end while their daughter sat in her room listening to the shouting, the screaming, and the crying. She would sit on her bed in near hysterics, wondering what she should or could do. Sometimes she feared for her mother, and she would try and work out what heavy object there was to hand that she could use to hit her father with if he really became violent. But she did not have to worry about her mother as it was usually her who

75

ended up on the receiving end of the violence. He would throw things at her if she attempted to intervene in their "discussions", throwing anything from a book to a chair. He always apologised prolifically afterwards, tears streaming down his face. The apology never made anything better, what she really wanted was her mother to stand up for her, for her mother to apologise.

She did try and talk to her father once about what was going on, but it did not do much good. The conversation had happened on the drive home from school, and her father had simply told her that she was to stop interfering. He said that his marriage and what went on between himself and her mother was none of her business. But she believed that it was her business. She was a product of that marriage and she had helped to cause the conflict by her revelations. Surely she had the right to try and help. She should have known better. The outcome of that particular conversation were bruises on her arms, an irate and irrational father, and a hysterical mother. She left home not long after, providence had it that it was time for university. She was glad to go.

Now all the cards were on the table and divorce seemed ever more likely. They claimed that they still loved each other but it was just not enough anymore. They could not even look each other in the face, there had been too much said and there was far too much guilt and confusion. She missed her daughter, she wished that she could go back and make things better, to be the mother that she had set out to be. And she missed her husband. She really was trying to make things work but she felt such a conflict of emotions that she didn't really know what to do for the best. She really needed someone to talk to, but she believed that no one would understand and that everyone would hate her if they knew exactly what had happened. Death was beginning to seem like the only way out. No one would miss her. In fact, she was certain that there would be people who would be pleased and relieved that she was gone: another problem out of the way. An overdose was not meant to be painful. She hoped not anyway. She did not want to go through any more pain.

Thoughts

You are my pièce de résistance, the crème de la crème.
That's what you said.
You whispered seductively in my ear:

You know serial killers who have ninety-nine victims and have that one who got away? Well, you're my number one hundred: the one who got away.

And they say romance is dead.

VII
Lost Content

Thoughts

Why do we as a species, continually strive for happiness? Happiness is elusive and it is transient. It is not a sustainable emotion. Instead, we should be striving for contentment, for our minds to be at peace. We should strive to be satisfied with what we have and with our circumstances. We should be easy in our minds and not complaining, opposing, or demanding. A satisfaction of mind without anxiousness or a craving for something else: this is what we should be reaching for.

The absence of craving or worry. Now wouldn't that be nice. To no longer complain and feel that inward discontent that preys on our spirit. To no longer hear that constant dissatisfied murmuring.

The Wife

Sadness, helplessness, and pessimism: these were the pervasive emotions that ran through her and so through her marriage. But deep down she knew that despite everything, she wanted to be with her husband, she wanted their relationship to survive. But she also wanted more.

She was anxious and could not sleep. Sex had not worked its soporific magic tonight and she found herself lost in thought again. She felt so worthless, and she had, over the years, retreated inside herself and almost lost all interest in life. Her negative thoughts deepened, and she truly felt that she was on the cusp of losing everything and everyone. She felt numb, empty, and despairing. She was terrified, and if her husband could have read her thoughts he would have been terrified too. As it was, he was simply angry. Angry that she was looking for attention and playing the victim—the spurned wife—as if she were the only one that was suffering. How dare she look for sympathy. She was not without blame by any means. They were both suffering, both tired of fighting, and both full of self-loathing and remorse for their actions. They both believed themselves to be useless, un-needed, and un-wanted. The shame and the guilt were overwhelming.

She felt tonight that if she could just find relief from all of that—the shame and the guilt—if she could just get away for a while then maybe things could be

alright. She didn't want to be around anyone—least of all her husband. He was so resentful, so full of anger and pain. How could she ever look him in the eye again? How could they carry on as if everything were fine? She wanted to run away, to go somewhere safe where she didn't have to pretend, but there was nowhere to go.

Then there was the voice. It had begun a long time ago. Taunting, humiliating, sneering. As time had passed, the voice, those thoughts, had become louder and more persistent.

You don't matter. This isn't going to last, no one would want to stay with you. Everyone would be better off without you. You're stupid, useless. You know that you hate waking up every morning, so why bother? Death is your only option left. You better do it. Now.

She began to think about ending it all, wiping the slate clean with a single act of self-destruction. She had begun to consider this option seriously. To plan. She pictured herself taking an entire bottle of pills washed down with alcohol. Sometimes she would find herself, catch herself off-guard, with a knife held absentmindedly to her wrist, as she prepared the evening meal. She would picture when and where she would end things. The thoughts, the images, and the voice, became more and more vivid with each passing day and she, in turn, became increasingly frightened. But she was not afraid of death. She was afraid of living.

And as she sat on the couch, waiting for sleep, her wedding album cradled in her lap, the voice continued to taunt her. Daring her to end it all.

Now would be a good time. This is it, just go ahead and do it. All you have to do is take the pills and go to sleep and it will all be over. Nothing hurts when you're dead.

The Woman

Wouldn't it be nice to be content? To just be happy with our lot?
How lame would the world be if we were all content with our current state?
I think it would be nice to be content.
No. You'd have no goal, no target. Just peace. Peace is boring. Peace is still.
How about happy if that were achievable?

There's no thrill in that. And what is "happy" anyway? It's so different for everyone.

I'm still working on a definition of "happy"...

It can't be defined.

I'm probably happy when I'm on my own, reading or out walking...

Maybe you don't even know happiness. What you describe is more like contentment or being relaxed. Happiness is when you have a rainbow in your brain!

I love that description! I think I'll use it!

Use away. That's what you do.

What? Seriously?

Yes. I'm annoyed again.

Don't be, please. You're my best friend and I love you.

I love you too but let's get real, no more bullshit. You only contact me when you need me or want something. You hide me away.

You hide me away too. You have never introduced me properly to your family and friends and you never will because you are a coward just like me and you don't want to mess up your existence either.

What the fuck! Really?

Now I'm annoyed too. I will never be anything other than a shadow in your life known only to you. I told my parents about you! Bet yours know nothing about me, not the truth that's for sure.

Ok...you're not being realistic. I've never hidden you, and I've never lied about you.

Does your mum or dad know about me? As in really know about me? I think not. That's a first. Made you quiet.

Thoughts

I wake up in the night punching and kicking. Once I woke up scratching and tearing at my wrists. To die, to sleep, perchance to dream—there certainly is the rub. Even in sleep I can't escape the voice, the torment, the constant murmuring.

If I were to die, would the voice follow, or would the rest be silence?

VIII
Holy Water and Garlic

The Patient

The room is non-descript. A cube. White walls and a small window set high in the wall. Two soft chairs face each other and in one corner is a small desk on which there is a laptop and a well-thumbed paperback book entitled "How to Boost Your Self-Esteem".

The man lounges in the soft chair which is placed under the window, his legs are crossed at the knee, his long fingers steepled. His dark hair is slicked tightly to his skull-like head and two gaudy, gold crucifixes are nestled at the collar of his pink shirt. He calmly surveys the woman, his patient, seated opposite him as she fiddles with a loose button on her coat. Finally he speaks, his voice soft and soothing and yet somehow commanding.

'Today's session will take an hour, an hour and a half. It is what I call a "developmental". I want a little background on you in order to get a better picture of what's going on and how I can help you. I have your doctor's file and the letter of referral of course,' he indicates a sheath of papers resting on his lap. 'But I want to hear it from you—you are after all the expert on the matter.'

She nods her head in assent. There are forms to be filled out first, the usual signing off to agree to bare one's soul at the understanding that all that goes on in this room is confidential, just between the two of them. Of course, she knows that this is nonsense. When she is gone, she is all too aware that the notes he makes will be transcribed onto the computer and filed away. He will use a number not her name of course, but the details will all be there: age, date of birth, address, medical history, transcripts of each session. All too easy to be found and traced back to her. And what about him, when he goes home and off-loads to his boyfriend, girlfriend, wife, husband, or significant other? And they in turn off-load, and they off-load, and they off-load? She decides she should be mindful of what she says, of what she discloses. She must try not to get too relaxed or too comfortable, to be lulled into a false sense of security. Opening up might well be beneficial but on the other hand...

He hands her a printed sheet. She has to mark her feelings—'a cross or a tick, it doesn't matter' he instructs—on a variety of statements. Do you have moments

of anxiety? Do you have panic attacks? Do you have difficulty sleeping? Do you find it hard to complete household tasks? Do you have difficulty in social situations? Do you like order and symmetry? Have you ever felt like harming yourself? The choice of answers—to cross or tick (it doesn't matter)—are not at all, sometimes, quite often, or all the time. The questions are extensive and varied. She wonders how she can answer them honestly, how this exercise can help. He must have noticed her uncertainty, her caution, because he begins to speak.

'Answer them in terms of how you have felt in the past seven days. There's no rush. Take your time,' he reassures.

She returns her attention back to the sheet of paper. The past seven days will be used to determine her mental health over the past few years. Correction: the past seven days will be used to determine her mental health from birth. Her responses today, marked with either a cross or a tick (it doesn't matter), will determine her sanity. *'How stupid,'* she thinks, *'that how I respond in this particular moment will have a lasting effect on how I will be forever viewed, on how I will be treated.'* How stupid, because how she responds in this particular moment could be completely different to how she may respond a minute from now, an hour from now, tomorrow, yesterday. But she continues to slash away (a tick, not a cross, it does matter), being as honest as possible in that moment, determined to be a willing and able student. To please. She hands the sheet back to him.

'Well done,' he says.

He says "well done" to almost everything that she says or does—she even got a "well done" for signing her name to the consent form. She feels like a small child. Maybe she'll get a sticker or a lollypop at the end of the session.

He goes on to ask the usual questions: names of parents, your relationship with them (fine); any siblings (an only child); married, divorced, single?

'Married,' she responds.

'Any children?' he queries.

'One,' she says nodding her head.

He comments on the beautiful choice of name, and she wonders, not for the last time, if he is working to a script.

'And how is your marriage?' he asks.

'It's difficult,' she admits. 'My daughter is all grown up and I—we—find that hard. The empty nest syndrome,' she laughs nervously and then pauses,

contemplating if she should make an admission, and eventually decides that she should. 'There has also been infidelity and I think—I don't know for sure—but it feels like the marriage is ending. That it has ended.'

'How does that make you feel?' he asks, his pen poised over his notepad.

'Scared and anxious. I'm not sleeping,' she hesitates briefly. 'And I feel like a failure, like I've wasted my entire life.'

He nods.

'What about externally, how do you feel in your body itself?' he asks.

'It makes me feel physically sick—'

'In what way?' he interrupts.

'I get headaches and stomach upsets. I get confused and forgetful too,' she admits.

They eventually get down to the nitty-gritty: her panic attacks, and the voice.

'Can you explain to me how you feel emotionally and physically, when you have these panic or anxiety episodes?' he asks, pausing to look up from his writing and to place his hand over his heart as he says the word "emotionally".

'Scared, breathless,' she replies. 'I get pins and needles in my hands.' She flaps her hands loosely as she says this before returning them to her lap.

'And what do you do?' he queries, looking directly at her, his eyebrows raised and his pen at the ready.

'What do you mean?' She feels confused.

'What do you do when you have these moments?' he asks. 'Think back. Go through it step by step for me.'

She takes a deep breath and closes her eyes before responding.

'I go and sit somewhere quiet, if I can, and try to slow my breathing,' she says. She opens her eyes, but does not meet his gaze, before continuing.

'I might try and distract myself—with a book, music, TV. If I'm out, I clutch something tightly—who I'm with, my bag, my hands. I leave marks on my skin.' She continues to find immense interest in the floor.

'I see,' he murmurs, writing in his pad. 'And what is the worst thing that could happen to you when you have these moments of anxiety?'

'I don't know. Nothing I guess,' she answers nervously, glancing at him quickly before looking away again. 'But sometimes they're worse. I lose sense of where I am, of what's happening.'

She pauses. It is hard to find the words. She looks him directly in the eye for the first time.

'Things move away,' she continues. 'I'd be say, looking at you and instead of you being three feet away you would suddenly be ten or twenty feet away.'

The words begin to tumble out of her.

'And I get confused. I can't tell reality from dreams or from the past or from memories,' she pauses briefly to collect her thoughts, to try and be more coherent. 'I keep having to ask someone to confirm what's real and what's not, what day it is, what year. It can last for hours. It's like I lose huge chunks of time.'

'I see,' he seems excited, his interest is definitely piqued. 'These flashbacks and the feeling of being out-of-body are what we call derealisation and dissociation. Derealisation is when things and people seem unreal, and dissociation is when we detach ourselves from many things. But we won't get too caught up in that yet, we'll leave that for another day.'

He pauses and she nods, making a mental note of the terms "derealisation" and "dissociation".

'So, what's the worst thing that can happen during one of these episodes?' he asks again.

'That I won't come back. That I'll be stuck not knowing what's real and what's not. It feels like I'm going mad,' she replies honestly. She feels anxious now, breathless and dizzy. The walls are visibly shifting, moving away, and the light is humming and lurid to her eyes.

'You are not going mad. You are obviously an intelligent woman. These are quite normal responses to stress and anxiety. Stress is very subjective, and it is intensely personal. Its effects are different for everyone,' he soothes. 'It is my job as the expert—not that I like to call myself that—' he laughs in a simpering fashion before resuming his speech. 'It is my job to help you deal with your current situation and your anxiety, and to take preventative steps to alleviate your stressors—both predictable and unpredictable—by adopting different stress management skills. Your family crisis of your daughter leaving home and the possibility of the end of your marriage has inevitably affected your quality of life, causing anxiety and panic attacks. We will work out how to manage these episodes using cognitive behavioural therapy, or CBT. But that's for another session. Today is about getting to know you.'

She nods and realises that not only has she been holding her breath, but that she is also holding the strap of her handbag so tightly that her knuckles are white,

and she can feel the indentations forming on the palms of her hands as her fingernails scythe her flesh. He must have noticed as he veers off script.

'Are you ok? You're doing really well,' he asks, a hint of worry to his voice.

'I'm just wondering how to get out of here,' she whispers.

He looks at her quizzically.

'I don't know how to get out,' she says, trying to stifle the rising panic which threatens to engulf her. 'I like to know about places before I get there—the layout. Exits, toilets, that kind of thing. Stupid I know.'

She definitely feels worried now. She has over-shared.

'That's ok. An escape route,' he laughs, but not in an uncaring way. 'Would you like me to show you out when we're finished?'

She nods and smiles weakly. She feels so stupid.

'Then that's what we'll do.' He smiles kindly before continuing abruptly. 'Voices. Do you hear them?'

He is back on script.

'Yes,' she responds immediately. 'But we all have that voice that we talk to, don't we?'

'Of course. Our inner voice, our conscious,' he agrees. 'What's yours like?'

'It depends. I'm always talking to it. Talking to me,' she taps the side of her head. 'I reason things out with me, with someone, with this voice. It's a constant dialogue. I find it hard to explain.'

'With whom?' he asks. 'Can you clarify please?'

'I suppose it's me that I'm talking to…I guess,' she replies. 'If something is worrying me, I have a little discussion with the voice inside here.' Again, she indicates the side of her head.

'And is this helpful?' he enquires.

'Sometimes. But I feel I do it too often. I'm always having an inner conversation or discussion. It's a constant buzz in my head. It never stops. I worry I'll get stuck in there.' She trails off.

'In where?' he prompts.

'In my head. I'll go crazy,' she replies. 'And sometimes the voice isn't just discussing things with me, it gets cross and angry. It scares me.'

'What does it say when it is cross and angry?' he asks gently.

'That I'm stupid. Worthless. That I should die,' she mumbles, looking at her hands that are currently twisting at the fabric of her coat.

'And have you ever tried to harm yourself?' he asks.

'No. Yes. I've thought about it,' she says. 'I had a knife. I held it to my wrist...'

Don't mention the other times, she tells herself.

'What stopped you?' he asks, looking at her intently.

She shrugs her shoulders and looks at the floor. She has been saying too much.

'And is there anyone you can talk to about this? Family? Friends?' he presses.

'I don't want to worry my family,' she says firmly.

'You worry about them?' he asks. 'Their feelings?'

'Yes. It's not fair to off-load my problems onto them,' she says decisively.

'And what about friends?' he asks as he continues to make notes.

'Friends?' she pauses. 'I...I don't have any.'

He continues to write for a few minutes before looking over his notes. He glances at his watch—a gold, cumbersome, tacky affair.

'Well. Time's nearly up,' he says. 'Would it be fair to say that you are feeling anxious and have low self-esteem?'

She nods and wonders where he got his qualifications—a lucky bag?

'In the next session,' he continues, 'we will try and find a cause for your anxiety and low self-esteem—because I believe that this is not just about your current situation—and we will work together to help you cope with difficult situations that trigger your anxiety.' He pauses and looks compassionately at her. 'I want to help you to learn to put you first, to stop worrying so much about other people's feelings. You are too caught up in negativity and you believe that you are no longer able to cope, but the reality is that you can.'

He smiles somewhat triumphantly before continuing.

'Ok!' he says with a sense of finality. 'Thank you so much for being so honest and open with me.'

He stands and escorts her to the door and helps her to find her escape route.

The Woman

I survived my first counselling session!

Well done!

Apparently I need cognitive behavioural therapy so I can manage my anxiety and learn to put myself first. Oh, and he said that I'm obviously an intelligent person.

Did you need a therapist to tell you that? I told you that a long time ago. And putting yourself first? How long ago did I tell you to do that? But sure…you never listen to me. I'm always trying to help you but what's the point? You don't listen to my advice; you don't do what I say. You make me so angry. Stop being a victim.

The Patient

'I've been studying our last few sessions and it is evident—please correct me if I am wrong—that the trauma you experienced in your childhood is a key factor in your current and very real problem of an anxiety disorder which has been triggered by your current marital issues and the departure of your only child from the family home,' he pauses, leaning back in his chair, awaiting her response which is not forthcoming. She is shocked. He went to college or university for this, is paid good money to tell her something that she already knows.

'It is now time to work on this, for you to set your SMART goals,' he continues when she remains silent. 'Now, I know you are wondering what SMART goals are, so let me explain. SMART is an acronym that stands for Specific, Measurable, Achievable, Realistic and Timely. So, the goals are "Specific", meaning that they are well-defined, clear, and unambiguous. They are "Measurable": they have specific criteria that measure your progress towards the accomplishment of the goal. They are "Achievable": we are not going to attempt the impossible! The goal we—you—set, you will be able to attain. They are "Realistic", within reach and relevant to your life purpose. They are "Timely", and by that, I mean that we will be setting a clearly defined timeline of how and when we—you—will achieve this goal. So basically, you are going to set yourself a SMART goal, something achievable that you can aim for which will improve the quality of your life. So, do you have any suggestions for a SMART goal?'

'The panic attacks. I want to stop them,' she replies at once.

'Ok, the panic attacks—the derealisation and dissociation episodes—are the main issues and you want them to stop,' he muses. 'I am afraid that I cannot do that for you, no more than I could get your enzymes to stop digesting food. Your panic attacks are a normal response to stress and to danger. It's your body's attempt at protecting you. But I can help you to manage or tolerate the panic attacks. Does that sound ok?'

'I guess so,' she replies, unsure.

'Good,' he says assertively. 'Now it seems to me that you worry too much about what others think of you, and of past situations. You cannot control that, so why try? You need to live in the present and appreciate what is good in your life. I want to enable you to differentiate between what is worth fighting for and what is not—to learn to let go of all that excess mental and physical baggage. I want to empower you, to make you strong enough to make your life better for you. I want you to stop avoiding, to stop using safety mechanisms—whether it be an action or a person. I want you to be in control, and all you need to do to achieve all of this is for you to make minor adjustments in your attitude and behaviour.'

He pauses to allow his words to sink in and then takes up the thread again.

'Let me use an analogy,' he says settling back into his chair and looking at her benevolently. 'In Romania—and this is the gospel truth—some people still passionately believe in vampires. So, every night before they go to bed, they sprinkle their sheets with holy water, put garlic around their beds, and wear crucifixes around their necks. In the morning, when they find themselves still human, they credit the holy water, the garlic, and the crucifixes for keeping them safe. Now, how do we let these people know that there are no vampires?'

'You take away the holy water, the garlic and the crucifixes, then they'll see that they never needed them in the first place.' She is not sure if he wanted an answer and now feels embarrassed.

'Exactly! The answer is we take away all those things, all those safety mechanisms—holy water, garlic, crucifixes—and show them that they were never needed,' he reiterates. 'It is a frightening and difficult course of action but one that is achievable and needed for their mental well-being. These people are suffering from stress because they are holding on to an unreasonable belief about living. Their belief in vampires is irrational. Life is more manageable and predictable when our expectations are realistic.' There is another brief pause. 'Like these people in Romania, you need to name and own your beliefs. This will be your first step in dealing with them. You also need to engage in reframing, a type of lateral thinking that helps us to search for alternatives—to recognise that there are so many ways in which to understand and perceive the same situation.'

He leans forward and gazes intently at her.

'So, this is what we are going to do with your SMART goals. Together, we are going to take away your holy water, your garlic, and your crucifixes.'

IX
Escape Route

The Wife

She stood beside the bed watching her husband as he slept. Her childhood and their youth together, it all seemed a lifetime away, as if it had happened to someone else. It all seemed so unreal. Only the wounds were still fresh and raw. They wept and oozed, never healing fully.

They had chosen each other and for tonight—for now—she was choosing this life. She persuaded herself that the affair had merely been a transgression, a scratching of an itch. It had meant nothing. It was really only words, nothing more. That was the official line and she had heard it repeated so often that she almost believed it herself now. What would be considered worse though? An affair that involved a physical relationship or an affair that never got passed the platonic stage? Or an affair that combined both the physical and the platonic? These were the thoughts that had seeped insidiously into their marriage as the years had passed.

It would appear though, that she had won. She had her husband, her marriage, and her home. But had she come first or had she simply won the consolation prize. They had been through so much together and they were still here, still hanging on. But what they were hanging onto exactly she was none too sure. Perhaps they could heal each other. But she no longer felt that she truly recognised the man lying in the bed. He was a stranger to her. She looked at her own dimly lit reflection in the mirror. She didn't recognise her either.

Thoughts

I am not what I was. My face has more lines. The laughter lines around my eyes I quite like, but not the hard lines around my mouth. They are like thick slashes of black pen from the sides of my nose to my lips. It is harsh, like bad stage make-up. I am beginning to resemble a ventriloquist's dummy.

While my face is gaunter and more world-weary, my body is softer and more malleable. I have acquired a stomach, rolls of soft, doughy flesh that oozes over my waistband and spills over the edge. It disgusts me. My legs are now tattooed with strange blue and purple designs. Delicate silver filigree has also appeared,

at the same time entrancing and repulsive. My veins are forming stars and tendrils as they push to the surface, and thick tortuous ropes encircle my ankles squeezing the flesh until it is bruised and decayed. The rest of my body is middle-aged, but my legs are embracing death.

I am not what I was. I look at myself and see a virtual stranger. I don't recognise myself. I don't know who I am. Maybe I never have.

The Wife

So here they were, just the two of them again. They had survived. They were surviving. A line had been drawn under the affair: they had both promised never to mention it again or to even allude to it. They had agreed to a fresh start, to try again. To forgive and forget. But could it ever be fully forgiven or completely forgotten.

She had got what she wanted: the safety and the security of marriage. But she was still dwelling on the negatives and tormenting herself over the past when it was the here and now that mattered, the endless possibilities that lay ahead. It was, however, these possibilities that terrified her—this new chapter in her life. It was just the two of them again. No one else to turn to for support or advice, for a shoulder to cry on. No child to focus all her attention on. Motherhood had defined her for so long—being a wife and being herself had come much lower down on her list of priorities. What would she do now? How would she cope.

She still felt so uncertain, she was unsure whether she had made the right decision. She had not got what she wanted exactly—she had got what she already had. And for that perhaps she should count herself lucky. But was it enough?

Thoughts

There is an ornamental cherry tree in our garden—a prunus accolade. It reaches to over eight feet high. It is a thing of beauty: rich, blood-red leaves in the autumn and in the spring, around easter-time, heavenly clusters of delicate pink blossoms.

Every spring I am mesmerised by the tree's exquisiteness, especially on a sunny day when the profusion of blossoms have a clear blue sky as a backdrop. When she was little, my daughter would ask to be lifted into the tree. There was a branch that was just perfect for her, and she would sit amongst the pretty petals. I have photographs of her perched in the tree. My very own flower fairy.

The voice says that the tree is perfect for me too. It says that I should hang myself from it. It doesn't say when I should do this, whether I should be a grotesque ornament to grace its bare branches in the winter or if I should opt for my favourite season, spring. Blue skies and pink blossoms. I could be a part of it all. The irony! Spring, the season of new life and me, dead.

The relief, the tranquillity that would bring.

But it wouldn't be fair on my family to see me like that, a hideous parody of my beautiful girl.

I told the voice I wouldn't. Not there.

I won that battle.

X
Can You Hear Me

Thoughts

Do you know what it's like to be alone? Do you know what it's like to be in love with someone who doesn't love you back? I am tired and empty and scared. I want your help, but I am afraid of your response. You used to love me, but you will never love me again when you realise just how fucked up I really am.

I do a lot of thinking. I can't help myself. I play scenes in my head over and over again, wondering how I could have done things better, and I practice the things that I want to say. The things that I should have said.

I have endless what ifs.

I am a failure. A disappointment. I know this.

I wish I could go back and start again, but I can't.

I'm sorry for all the pain I've caused and for hurting you. But I'm hurting too. I'm tired of all the yelling and all of the pretending. I'm tired of remembering. I'm just so tired.

Sometimes I wonder if I died, would anyone care?

The Woman

Hey babe. How are you? I'm missing you way too much.

Hey. Miss you too.

Is everything ok? I'll try and see you soon. I promise.

No pressure. It's ok.

You haven't contacted me for a while. I thought you might have replaced me...

You are irreplaceable. It's hard to replace that one text a week, a brief meeting now and then...

Very funny. I know this isn't exactly what we wanted. It's frustrating for me too. I do love you.

Love you back.

Thoughts

The best ways to commit suicide in no particular order.

Option one: overdose. But which tablet? Can paracetamol kill you? They would be easy to get, I'd just have to go to a few pharmacists in order to get enough. Apparently twenty-four grams of paracetamol is generally accepted to be a fatal overdose, so twenty-four to thirty tablets should do the trick. But it would probably be better if I mixed different tablets, say easy to get over the counter medication—Tylenol, ibuprofen, cough or cold medicine, antihistamines. Anti-depressants are supposed to be quite effective too if combined with alcohol or painkillers or both, and I have them. They say that you also have to consider weight to tablet ratio—that's lethal dose in relation to body weight. It would be handy if I could get hold of class A drugs like heroin, cocaine, or methadone.

So, the correct amount of a mix of tablets combined with alcohol should do the trick. But I could improve on this method by putting a plastic bag over my head. I'd have to make sure that the bag wouldn't tear, and I would probably need a seal—maybe an elastic band would work. It's meant to be a lethal but painless way of going, and it leaves a peaceful looking body. I would need to put the bag over my head as the drugs and alcohol took effect—but would I have time, and would I be able? What if instinct kicked in and I rip the bag off my head? Then of course, there's the risk of survival with kidney failure, irreversible liver failure, half a mind trapped in a useless body, or worse still, an entire mind trapped, caught in an endless spiral of thoughts with no escape. Maybe not an overdose then.

Option two: slitting my wrists. Very gruesome. My intense dislike of blood might be an issue—I would probably faint at the first miniscule droplet. However, in theory I should imagine it is easy to do if fully committed, and I certainly wouldn't have a problem finding a knife. But is one wrist enough? Because I am assuming that once you've done the first one you might not have the strength to switch hands and start sawing away on the opposing wrist. And are the cuts horizontal or vertical? Which would be more effective? I'm getting light-headed just thinking about this option. Maybe not the best route.

Option three: hanging. Quite horrible although possibly quick. It's meant to be simple to do, and the materials needed are readily available and so easy to obtain. But I guess that would depend on the rope and the knot. Maybe I could get a book on knot-tying. I think I would need to learn to tie a running knot or

slip knot. That shouldn't be too hard but then think how long it took me to learn to tie my shoelaces…And then where would be a good place to do it? And do I go for a short drop or a drop hanging? Decisions, decisions.

Apparently you see flashing lights and hear ringing sounds when you hang. That doesn't sound too bad. If carried out correctly, hanging should work, but so much could go wrong: the rope could snap leaving me with serious injury, brain damage or a fractured spine; or I might be found before I die. It seems it can take anything from three to forty minutes to die from hanging—thirteen seconds to three minutes to lose consciousness, just over a minute to lose muscle tone, another four minutes or so for muscle movements to stop. So hanging will be slow. My face will be red and bulging, my eyes will protrude, and my tongue will be thrust out, stuck between my clenched jaws. As I hang, no doubt instinct will kick in and I will try to free myself, I will claw at my neck and thrash violently. It will be gruesome and horrific. There is no glamour to this death.

Option four: I could shoot myself. That's probably the most effective form of suicide—a sure-fired solution if you pardon the pun. A bullet to the brain. I'd be dead before I even registered the gunshot. I'd just need to get a gun and some bullets. A shotgun would be the most effective firearm as when it's fired at the chest the shot would spread out and should cause death; but if I tried to aim for the head—no that wouldn't work. Then there's buying a gun, that could prove difficult and raise a lot of unwanted attention. Also, although it is the most lethal and reliable way of killing oneself, nothing is ever one hundred per cent—what if I miss my heart or the right part of my brain? There would be no death just very unpleasant injuries.

Option five: I could jump from a height. That could be effective. From what I've read online, I would need to jump from a hundred and fifty feet or higher on land, and two hundred and fifty feet or higher on water. Additionally, ideally, I would need to land on my head in order for it to work, especially if jumping from a lower height. Tricky. Perhaps I could find a suitable bridge? What if I changed my mind mid-drop, it doesn't bear thinking about, and if the bridge wasn't high enough, I might survive with excruciating injuries and be even more of a burden—a disappointment—to everyone. Shattered bones and internal organ damage instead of death? No thanks.

Option six: jumping in front of a high-speed train. Now there's an idea. It definitely would have to be high speed; it couldn't be a train that is slowing down to pull into the platform. The only thing is the trauma my death would cause for

any onlookers and for the train driver. That wouldn't be fair. And what about me, my death? As long as I lost consciousness quickly then my death should be quite painless, but if not…it would be horrific. Not a train then.

Option seven: drowning. I could be like Ophelia, mermaid-like, crowned and garlanded with flowers, singing until I reached a muddy death. Like in the painting by Millais. But again, would instinct kick in? Would I fight for breath and try to reach the surface or the shore? Maybe if I combine it with alcohol and with tablets? It's a possible winner.

Option eight: carbon monoxide. The so-called "sweet death", sweet because as you inhale the carbon monoxide you simply slowly drift off to sleep, unable to react or to move. Or so they say. Car exhaust fumes would be the handiest way, I could run the car engine continuously in the garage or run a pipe from the exhaust directly into the car. But my car is quite new, I'd probably need an older car to ensure high enough levels of carbon monoxide. And when they say a slow death, translate that as anything from five to fifteen minutes of gasping for air and vomiting as my eyes pop. Not so sweet then. And if I am discovered, if I survive, I could face brain damage, memory loss (maybe that wouldn't be so bad), heart problems, blindness, psychosis, or paralysis. One to think about I suppose.

Option nine: poisoning. Now that's quite a romantic option in its own way. I could use propofol if I could get my hands on it. Or cyanide. Cyanide would be hard to get and there are mixed reviews for the cyanide option—it's either painful or miserable, it is either quick or takes up to eleven minutes. Injecting potassium chloride (you can buy this stuff online so easily) is more lethal than cyanide but I would have to work out the lethal minimum dose—get it wrong and I would just blister up and be in excruciating pain. I could combine potassium chloride with sedatives though, but either way it wouldn't be a particularly peaceful or painless death.

Then of course there is arsenic. I quite like that idea. Very nineteen-forties film noir, and very literary—think Du Maurier's Rachel and her ominous stash of laburnum seeds. I don't have a laburnum in the garden but there are other plants that could do the trick. Our Lady's gloves, Our Lady's thimbles, fairy bells, fairy's glove, bloody man's fingers, witch's thimble, dead man's bellows—all names for digitalis purpurea or the common foxglove as it's more commonly known. I have it growing in the garden, it is a magical plant with drooping flowers in soft shades of purple covered with maroon spots surrounded

by a white ring, the white ring acts as a honey guide for bees. A beautiful plant that hides a violent medicine. The leaves contain the deadly poison cardiac glycosides, which increase the output force of the heart and the ingestion of which can lead to a heart attack and even death in some cases. And these toxins are not just in the leaves, they are present throughout the plant, root, and seeds; but it is just before the seeds ripen that the foxglove is at its most poisonous. Too little ingested would just cause a headache, nausea, skin irritation, and diarrhoea. Too much—or the right amount, depending on your viewpoint—would slow the heart rate so much that the brain would be starved of oxygen. The bodies reflex response in this scenario will be to try and increase the heart rate, and it's this response that will eventually lead to a heart attack. Ironically foxglove is actually used in cardiac treatment, so it can heal a heart as well as stop one. As they say, 'The dose makes the poison.' It could work. I could make a cocktail—some foxglove leaves, a little mint, some gin—and have myself a very special cocktail party for one. So long as I didn't vomit it all up.

And last but not least option ten: I could use the best poisons of all, always readily available—hopes, dreams, love, and last but not least, life. They will definitely kill me and there is no way to stop them either. The only problem is that they are extremely slow, and it will be a lingering and agonising death.

The Woman

I've been thinking about you.
Really?
Yes. When I'm burning calories...
What the fuck! Why are you telling me this? Why would I want to know that?
Sorry.
I don't know what's worse, his situation or mine.
We're all fucked one way or another.
Yeah. You're fucking me mentally.
Maybe one day...
I've heard it all before.
Fair enough.
I challenge you.
Challenge accepted.
I didn't say what the challenge was! I'll tie you up and spank your ass.
Promises promises.

I will keep my promise. And I do need your love. In all ways.

Thoughts

Hallo? Can you hear me? Can you see me? Is the pain in my eyes so undeniable? Can't you see my tears? I wish you would help me. I need you. I can't cope anymore.

Don't you realise that the pain is eating me away? I am so afraid. Please don't turn away, I need to know you. I wish you would listen to me. I want to scream at you to get your full attention, but the screams are caught like snared animals in my throat.

Are you really listening to me? Do you really understand me? I'm dying inside but you can't see that can you? All I need is for you to show me that you genuinely care. For you to pull me through. To love me.

I need someone to hold me and tell me that everything is going to be all right. This world frightens me so much. My life is so lonely. There's no one that I can turn to, yet I feel closed in, suffocating.

Can you exorcise my demons? Can you free me from my cage? I am forever reaching out for you, but you are always just out of reach. Distant. A dream.

Why won't you help me? Can't you hear me? Why aren't you listening? Please don't push me away.

Please. Help me.

XI
We Are What We Remember

Thoughts

Every day I put on a smile and I hide my problems from you. I don't talk to you because I don't want to worry you, because I don't want to lose you. And how can I confide in you? You wouldn't understand. I don't like myself. I hate me. I am disgusting. Abhorrent. A fuck-up. If I can't be happy with myself, then how can anybody else?

But I'm tired of feeling unloved. I'm tired of no one caring. But most of all I'm tired of pretending to be happy.

The Woman

Hey! How's your day? I wouldn't mind getting my hands on you.
How would you do that?
I'm not sure.
I'm not surprised.
But if I did get my hands on you, I'm sure we'd have fun.
Right. You keep saying that. You've been saying that for years.
I'll escape soon and we won't put ourselves under pressure like we did before.
Ok. I'll be here waiting.
Good. Love you.
Love you back.

The Lover

She fumbles in her handbag for her phone. He was supposed to get back to her but there is still no word. She scrolls down to his number and hesitates for a fraction of a second before pressing call.

'Hey,' his voice is low and sleepy sounding.

'Hey, what's up?' she replies, concerned by his lack of enthusiasm.

'I'm not having a great day. I'll catch you another time,' he responds.

'What's wrong?' She's really worried now, worried and disappointed.

'I just don't feel too great,' his words are heavy and leaden. 'Where are you?'

'I managed to get away!' she responds, all too aware that she is beginning to sound whiny. *'Please don't let me cry,'* she thinks.

'What are you going to do now?' he asks, concern creeping into his voice.

'I'm not sure. Just wander around I guess,' her voice trails off.

'You can't do that,' suddenly he sounds determined and more awake. 'Come over.'

'It's fine. Don't worry,' she replies, thinking as she says it that it is not fine, they had a date, and please worry.

'Yes. Come over,' he repeats.

'Are you sure?' she asks as she walks towards his house, not bothering to wait for his reply.

'It's fine. Come,' he says with finality.

'Ok. If you're sure. I won't stay long. See you soon,' she says and hangs up.

She finds herself at his door in record time, breathless and flustered, and is even more so when he opens the door.

'Hi,' she says, smiling nervously as he reaches down to embrace her in his strong arms. 'Are you feeling any better?'

'I'm happy now,' he responds, and the biggest smile lights up his face.

Safely ensconced in his kitchen she sits at the table.

'Tea? Sugar?' he offers.

'Yes please,' she responds. 'But no sugar, I'm sweet enough.'

'Says who?' he laughs.

They sit facing each other across the kitchen table, each nursing their mugs of tea. They talk, a little nervously at first—she's shy and he's unsure of how to play things. They put the world to rights, discussing politics and the environment. They talk about TV and movies. Eventually the topics get more intimate, and they move on to their fantasies.

On impulse, driven by a force that feels outside of her and out of her control, she stands and goes to him. She sits on his knee and runs her fingers through his greying hair, gazing into his soulful brown eyes. He wraps his arms around her waist.

'Is this your idea of jumping me?' he whispers, a smile playing on his lips.

'More like squashing you!' she laughs and kisses him.

Gently, expertly, he removes her top and slips down her bra. He begins to kiss and suck at her nipple until it is hard in his mouth. Then, sighing deeply, he re-dresses her. He rests his head on her chest and she tenderly kisses the top of

his head before moving onto his neck and nibbling at his ear. She cups his face in her two hands and his eyes meet hers, eyes that are alight with passion. He kisses her, his tongue hard and forceful, and she pulls back slightly—suddenly nervous and unsure. He expertly manoeuvres her until she is sitting on his lap with her back to him. He nuzzles and kisses her neck sending shivers of pleasure down her spine. He fondles her breasts and then moves his strong hands to her hips, gently but firmly moving her rhythmically into his groin. He sighs and moans.

'Talk dirty to me,' he whispers gruffly.

She is caught off guard. She freezes momentarily, both mentally and physically.

'I can't,' she falters. 'I don't know how. I'm too shy.'

She feels so stupid. Out of her depth.

'Would you really fuck us both?' he persists.

'Yes,' she replies quietly, and he responds with a deep animalistic moan.

'I'll tie you up and keep you for a week,' he breathes into her ear. And then suddenly he stops, alert and on guard like an animal aware that it is about to become someone else's dinner.

'She's back,' he says.

'What?' she gasps, panicked.

'She's home!' he says more urgently, pushing her off his lap. She quickly returns to her seat across the table and her now cold cup of tea.

His wife enters the kitchen and says a curt hallo before making her excuses and disappearing upstairs.

'Is she ok?' she asks nervously. 'Am I causing problems by being here?'

'No, it's not you,' he says glibly, all fear now apparently gone. 'We're arguing. But it's ok, she's fine with polygamy. Threesomes are good for everyone's sex life,' he says with a laugh.

Is he serious? She isn't sure.

'Stay a bit longer,' he urges. 'Chat a bit.' He pauses, assessing her mood.

'What do you think of her?' he asks, nodding his head in the direction that his wife went.

'She's nice,' she answers demurely.

'I didn't mean it like that.' There is a brief pause while he thinks. 'Do you like women? Have you ever been attracted to them?'

'Yes,' she replies immediately, voicing her true feelings for the first time and shocking not only him but herself also.

'Seriously? When? How?' he falters.

'Always I guess,' she replies, her eyes studying the cup that she holds in her hands. She doesn't want to discuss this right now, it's all too much. She has known for some time, always has, like she said, but had only really become aware of these feelings and began to truly accept them recently.

'What about the three of us?' he asks cautiously. 'It would be good—good for us all. Will you at least think about it?'

She looks away feeling awkward and confused.

'Only if you want to,' he reassures her. 'Consider it.'

She smiles and nods briefly, and sensing that her shutters are coming down he changes the subject.

'Why did you like me in the first place?' he asks. 'Was it because I like music and poetry and the stars?'

He is teasing her, but he has put her at ease again. They both laugh.

'Did you like me straight away?' he presses.

'No,' she responds bluntly and is met by a look of disappointment—mock or real, she isn't quite sure.

'I liked you,' she continues, 'after a while. Because you noticed me. People don't normally. And because you made me feel—'

'Please don't say special,' he interrupts. 'You know you're special. And so beautiful.'

She smiles shyly before asking him the same question.

'And why did you like me?'

'Because you helped me,' he says candidly. 'When you thought I was in trouble or sad, you always tried to help. No one else did.'

Instinctively, as one being, their hands reach out across the table, and they stroke and caress each other's entwined fingers. His fingers she notices, are strong and smooth, his nails are perfectly manicured. For a second, she feels embarrassed by her own care-worn hands, the dry skin, and the chipped nails. She pulls away. It is time to go. Reluctantly he escorts her to the front door and they embrace, holding each other tightly, her head nestled on his chest.

'See you next month?' he laughs, but he is only half joking. He hates how they rarely get to see each other.

She stands on tiptoe to reach his cheek and kisses him.

'I'll see you soon,' she says.

As she walks away the warm glow, the feeling of worth he always imbues her with, slowly dissipates. She tries to focus on the memory of him—his face, his voice, the touch of his hands. When she was in a reflective mood, or upset, his face would always mirror hers, and he would be concerned and he would search for ways to help her, to make things better. And invariably he did make things better. It was at times like having her very own personal counsellor. Likewise, when she was feeling frivolous and playful, when she was making lewd and suggestive comments—in short when she was in self-destruct mode—his face would light up and that boyish grin that she loved so much, would illuminate the room. And when he was feeling passionate his face was almost a mask. He was intense. Focused. Almost aggressive.

She wondered which version of him she preferred, which version she wanted most, and she came to the conclusion that she needed all three of him.

The Woman

You were so kind and sexy and handsome yesterday. You left me wanting more. It's torture. I can't wait to see you again.
Not talking?
I am.
Good. I miss you. I want you...
No response?
No response is a good thing. It means that I agree with everything you say.
Good. Not that I believe you for a second. You're just a typical man ignoring my messages. Love you.
Ha ha. Love you back.
You know that I will overthink that right? You said that no response was a good thing and now you've responded...

*

Can I ring?
Now's not a good time. Sorry.
You're never there when I need you. I'm always here for you whenever you feel the need to open a stupid phone app. I'm sick of virtuality. Leave me alone.

This is the best that I can do at the minute. Talk to me. Maybe I can help. Please don't think that I'm playing games. I'm not. If I could see you every day, I would. Texting isn't enough you're right, but it's better than nothing at all. I'd be lost without you. I love you.

I love you too. I'm sorry.

It's ok. I know that I can seem distant and that I can be selfish. I know that you have your own things to deal with. I hope you're ok.

I'm ok. I'm just under pressure with domestic stuff and I feel like your life is moving on while I'm stuck here.

You should know by now how much you mean to me and the fact that I haven't been able to see you doesn't change that one bit. Please remember that I love you.

I love you too.

*

I hope to see you soon.

Ok.

You're so eager.

There's nothing to be eager about.

Whatever.

Exactly.

I shan't bother you anymore then.

Perfect.

I figured that you'd lose interest in me eventually.

It's like I said before, you're never here when I need you. You'll probably only see this message the day after tomorrow. So what's the point?

I know that it's frustrating when we don't get to see each other. You think I don't get upset about that? You have to tell me if you need me. I'm not psychic. You mean a lot to me, you know that, but things aren't ever that easy or ever that black and white.

I'm just so annoyed with all the "I'll see you soon" and then nothing ever happens.

Just let me know what you want to do. I love you and I don't want to lose you, but I understand if you want to end things.

So am I no longer persona non gratis?
What's the point? You're harmless. Hardly any danger.
True. How are you?
I'm good. You? All ok?
Yes, I'm good. I have counselling today.
That's good. You have to be positive and talk and be honest.
Ok.
Call into me for a chat one day.
I will.

The Lover

She rings the doorbell. There's no answer. Has he forgotten? Suddenly she is overwhelmingly anxious. Then the door opens and there he is, hair tousled after a quick shower, looking athletic and handsome in shorts and a T-shirt. He pulls her to him and quickly shuts the door. They kiss, his tongue probing and exploring her as he grabs her face, her breasts, her bottom. He leads her upstairs to the bedroom where, laid out neatly on the bed is a skirt and a top. Carefully, reverently, he moves this reminder of his wife from the bed before turning his attention to removing her clothes and then his own.

He sucks her breasts hard and then pushes her forcefully onto the bed, and the next thing that she knows is his huge, hard penis is inside her mouth. She is hungry for him after all this time. She sucks and she licks, one hand firmly on the shaft moving backwards and forwards, the other caressing his balls, until she nearly chokes on the size of his tumescence.

'I want to take you from behind. Can I?' he asks gruffly.

'Yes,' she consents, but she is not fully committed to the idea. 'Ok.'

She kneels on the bed, and he slips inside her.

'Feel your pussy,' he commands as he slaps her firm bottom.

'Harder,' she gasps quietly. 'Harder.' But his slaps are still too soft.

He pulls out and comes, catching the milky spray in his discarded T-shirt.

'Did you come?' he asks, breathlessly.

'No,' she replies, disappointed and frustrated. She feels let down. 'You should have spanked me harder.'

'Why didn't you say?' Now it is his turn to feel upset and frustrated. 'I would have. And I would have waited.'

'I did ask,' she replies as she pulls on her clothes. 'But don't worry. There's always the next time.'

They kiss and lie facing each other on the rumpled sheets, she fully dressed, he still bare-chested.

'You're so sexy,' she sighs. He blushes as she continues. 'It's funny, but I don't feel guilty at all. I thought that I would. But after all my worries about doing this, it just felt right.'

She pauses before continuing, averting her gaze from his ever-penetrating stare.

'I hope that I wasn't a disappointment,' she says coyly.

'You're never a disappointment,' he whispers, and leaning forward he gently kisses her neck.

Then he moves back and is suddenly more business-like, although there is still a certain sensitivity, an undertone of pleading.

'I just want more from you. You're beautiful and clever, and I want you to be the best you can be. I know that you have a lot of obstacles in your path, but you just need to be more assertive, do things for you for a change, stand up for yourself. I don't want to change you…'

The unspoken "but" hovers and lingers, as does her unspoken response: this is me; this is who I am, want me for me, love me as I am.

*

Later that day he leans into his wife, wrapping his arms around her waist, a smile playing on his lips, and he whispers seductively, 'I've been a naughty boy.'

The Woman

I hope it's ok to call you.

Of course. Is everything ok?

Yes. I just miss you. I wanted to hear your voice.

Ok…why don't you come over?

I can't. I only have a few minutes…

The same old story. When are you going to take control of your life and put yourself first for once?

I am trying. It's hard.

You're not trying. Get a job, join a club, make friends. I hate thinking of you locked up in your little cage.

You don't understand—

I do. You constantly overthink and you won't allow yourself to feel. You didn't even let go when we had sex! You were like a statue! I didn't know what I was supposed to do. After all those stories that you told me…

It's difficult! Please try and understand! I rang because I miss you and all you do is have a go at me! This was meant to be a nice conversation and I end up feeling sadder. You're so intimidating when you get cross…

Look, I'm sorry. I'm real, I'm just expressing what I think that you should do to live your life in a happier way. But if I make you sad, don't ring anymore.

You know that I don't want to do that…I'll text you later, ok? I love you.

Ok. Bye.

*

I'm sorry for what I said yesterday. I want to try and explain. It's not so much that I'm intimidated by you as that I am intimidated by your honesty, and I do really appreciate that honesty by the way.

I'm going to be real for you now. I was going to say this face to face but I'm too much of a coward to do that—plus you would probably interrupt! So. You always want to know what's going on inside my head and why to you I seemed so detached when we had sex. I only opened up about this recently, so this is extremely hard for me, and I haven't told anyone the full details, but here goes. From about age six to eleven, I was abused. Sexually. I went from happy and confident to scared and quiet and full of self-loathing. That personality, that idea of myself, it has kind of stuck.

I've kept the abuse locked away but occasionally it rises to the surface and affects me. I never expected that I would be—could be—wanted or loved. And sometimes I find it hard to let go during sex—it feels wrong, and I feel guilty enjoying it. When we tried, please know that I wanted you. You did nothing wrong. I just felt overwhelmed.

I know that I need to confront the abuse in order to get over it but it's very hard. I've hidden it for so long. But it's resurfacing more frequently now, and I realise

that perhaps if I confront it, then maybe I would be less likely to be a victim in other areas of my life.

I do want you. I have for such a long time. I never expected that you would want me too. I fell in love with you and that scares me—allowing myself to feel, to love more than one person.

Anyway. Maybe that was too real for you, but it might help you to understand me and why I struggle sometimes. I understand if now you want to walk away.

*

Running yet?

No. No reason to. I am so sorry about what happened to you. Call into me tomorrow? I'll make you tea and we can talk.

Sorry if I over-shared. You're so honest and I wanted to be honest too. I was worried what you might think.

No need to be worried.

Thank you. It was hard to tell you, but I hope that it explains…but I don't want your pity…and I hope you're not disgusted by me now.

Please. Stop.

Sorry.

As I said, no need. Stop apologising.

I nearly said sorry again. I'll see you tomorrow. Love you.

Love you back.

Thoughts

Our entire lives we are told what to think, what to feel, what to say. We are told how we should behave. We are told who we are. All those personas we are given. I am a wife, a mother, a friend, a lover, a daughter, a colleague. But who am I really? What do I really think and believe? I have lost myself. Assuming that I was ever "found" in the first place.

I don't know who I am. I am lost. We are all lost in the end though. Lost with endless thoughts of "what if" and "if only"—a constant flow of regret.

XII
Fight or Flight

The Patient

She sits in her usual chair, the man—her therapist, counsellor, or psychiatrist, he has yet to explain his role—is seated across from her. She notes that although his trousers and shirts change—today the shirt that he is sporting is a silky striped, purple affair—the jacket always remains the same crumpled beige linen blazer.

'Today I would like you to demonstrate what you do when you feel anxious, when you feel a panic attack or a derealisation episode is about to happen,' he announces.

'What do you mean?' She fidgets awkwardly, fiddling with the remains of a tissue in her coat pocket, shredding it to pieces.

'When your heart rate increases and you are feeling afraid, you go to your safe place,' he pauses briefly. 'And what do you do, in that safe place?'

'I breathe,' she replies. 'In through the nose, out through the mouth.'

'Show me,' he commands.

She sits upright in her chair and attempts to demonstrate, but after a few breaths she stops. She feels silly.

'And does this breathing help?' he enquires. 'What does it achieve?'

'It calms me down. It sometimes can stop my panic attack,' she replies.

'What would happen if you didn't do this—this breathing exercise?' he asks.

'I don't know,' she pauses, thoughtful. 'I guess I'd have a full-on panic attack.'

The man considers her reply for a moment before continuing.

'And why would that be bad?' he probes.

'It would be scary, frightening. I might end up having—what did you call them? A derealisation or dissociation episode,' she says.

'And what is the worst thing that could happen if that occurred?' he queries, tilting his head on one side, his fingers steepled. She wonders if he practices this concerned counsellor pose in the mirror every morning before coming to work.

'It could be dangerous,' she replies, pulling herself back to the here and now.

'Of course it won't be,' he answers decisively.

He is smiling now, the smile and his tone verging on the condescending.

'Yes, it could be,' she says firmly. 'I could be crossing a road and get knocked down. What if I was driving a car? Minding a child? And I lose focus? I lose my grip on reality? I forget where I am and what I'm doing? It is dangerous!'

She is angry now—he doesn't seem to understand. The man looks momentarily confused and shocked, either by her outburst or by the fact that his topic has been strayed from. He had not factored in this type of response; she has drifted away from the line of enquiry that he had planned on pursuing. He shuffles his notes peremptorily and clears his throat. There will be no deviation today.

'From my formulation last week,' he declares, choosing to completely ignore her response and her obvious worries regarding her panic and anxiety and all that comes with it. 'I've come up with a few ideas.'

He leans forward and she mirrors his movement. He produces a piece of paper. On it is a diagram, a photocopy from a textbook. She peers at the paper and notes that the man is not competent at photocopying: the image is off-centre and far too dark to be easily discernible.

'This diagram—this cycle,' he says earnestly, 'I feel that it explains what happens to you when you have a panic attack or a derealisation or dissociation episode. Let me talk you through it.'

He pauses to retrieve a pen from his desk.

'"It felt unreal",' he reads, scrawling a red line under the first heading. 'Follow the arrow and we have "what if I panic?" This leads to "feeling scared or anxious".'

She nods. They obviously teach counsellors—therapists, psychologists, whatever title it is he gives himself—the art of stating the bloody obvious.

'This leads to,' he continues, again indicating the pertinent parts by underlining in red pen, '"shaking, heart racing, breathless, unreality".'

Another pause before recommencing. He obviously believes he is onto something momentous, something ground-breaking. She, however, is finding it increasingly hard to concentrate and to feign interest.

'And this is where your safety behaviours come in,' he says, scrawling the words "safety behaviours" and an arrow next to the printed words "deep breathing, tried to relax". He continues to speak.

'Safety behaviours such as turning to a specific person for support or doing your deep breathing and so on.'

She nods again and he continues in a soft, patronising manner, referring once more to the piece of paper and its diagram.

'You can see that this behaviour leads two ways: to more panic—it says on the diagram "I'm having a heart attack", but in your case your catastrophic interpretations are "I won't come back, I'm going mad"…' He hesitates and says, half to himself, 'Let me just write that down on the diagram,' before resuming his explanation.

'Or there is a second route: back to the shaking and the heart-racing. It is a cycle. These safety behaviours are just avoidance,' he clarifies. 'We are back to the crucifixes and the holy water, remember? You need to get rid of them.'

He smiles triumphantly.

'I don't agree,' she responds, feeling suddenly and uncharacteristically brave. 'If I do my deep breathing, then the anxiety—the fear—it goes away. I'm safe and those around me are safe. If I let the panic attack run its course, if I let the fear take over—then I am helpless, I'm not in control. Who knows what could happen?'

He looks slightly disappointed and offended by her reaction, but he continues, only now he is advocating the safety behaviours.

'Yes, the deep breathing—your safety behaviours—they can be helpful especially if out and about in the supermarket and so on,' he says. 'Taking a sip of a hot or cold drink is also an excellent way of grounding oneself in order to prevent a panic attack. Holding an object can also be effective.'

He takes his mobile phone out of the pocket of his linen jacket and holds it out to her.

'Here,' he says. 'Hold this. Feel it. Tell me about it.'

She is perplexed. She does not want to touch his phone, but obedient as usual she takes it and looks at it, holding it loosely in her lap. All she can think is, where has it been? Does he wash his hands properly, or at all? It has been against his ear, his waxy cheek, his gelled hair. Disgusting. But she tries. She wants to please.

'It's rectangular. Smooth,' she murmurs as she looks at the phone, moving it awkwardly in her hands.

'What about the edges or the texture of the phone?' he prompts.

'Is it hot? Cold?'

'The edges are rounded and it's not particularly cold,' she responds decisively.

She has nothing more to say and continues to hold the phone loosely in her lap, avoiding eye contact. She wonders what she is meant to do now. Should she interrupt him and pass the phone back to him or stand and place it on his desk. Eventually she decides to keep hold of the phone until the end of the session. It is safer that moving or making unsolicited conversation.

'Homework!' he declares brightly. 'Well, not really homework,' he corrects himself, 'but some notes to help you and an exercise.'

He produces two postcards from inside his file, one with writing on one side and one with writing on both sides. She observes that the pen he used to write these postcards with is black, and the handwriting is spidery with not much pressure used. She also notes that the writing is difficult to read. Perhaps he wrote them in a hurry. He begins to read them to her in a singsong and somewhat condescending manner.

'"Things to do when I feel panicky: read through my therapy notes"—that's the other card, we'll come to that in a minute—"focus my attention on my thoughts in my head; or"…'—a meaningful pause during which she notes that the "or" has been printed in capital letters and underlined twice—'…"or don't do anything and see how long it lasts".'

He pauses again for dramatic effect or perhaps he is expecting more belligerence on her part.

'So, this is your homework. It's a behavioural experiment,' he explains before continuing to read from the card.

'"To test out over the next week what will happen if I drop my safety behaviours and tolerate",'—she notices the underlining of this last word—'…"my anxiety".'

Another triumphant pause.

'What do you think?' he asks.

'I think that it sounds scary and difficult,' she responds honestly. 'But I will try.'

'Good. Now the second card.' He puts the first card to one side and as before, he holds the second card out between them. 'I find that most patients keep this card with them, or have it pinned up somewhere—on the fridge perhaps—as it can be of help. These are your "rational responses", your therapy notes to read when you feel panicky.'

He reads to her:

'"This is anxiety, I cannot"…'—again she notes that the word "cannot" is underlined—'…"I cannot lose control or go crazy; I have had loads of these panic attacks in the past and I was ok; it is a temporary increase in blood pressure, it is designed to protect me".'

She wonders if he realises his contradictions: lose the safety behaviours one minute only to replace them with a different set of safety behaviours the next, in this case a safety behaviour in the form of a card to read and to keep on her person. He hands her both of the postcards and they both lean back in their chairs.

'Your panic is designed to protect you,' he repeats in a firm voice. 'These anxiety attacks, these derealisation episodes, are your fight or flight responses. They are normal. The human race would have been wiped out long ago if they were any harm to us. If you had a heart attack, the doctor would inject you and you would let him, yes?'

'Yes,' she replies.

'And they are injecting you with—what?' he queries.

'Adrenaline I think,' she says, unsure.

'Exactly,' he responds. 'It gets the heart beating. And it is adrenaline that causes your panic attacks. They are nothing to fear.'

She is still not convinced. She ponders that it is a shame that he can't experience one of her derealisation episodes, so that he can understand that her fear is real, so that he can experience the lack of control, the confusion. He sees her uncertainty and continues once again, this time trying a different tack.

'Let me use an analogy.' He adjusts his position in his chair and crosses his legs. 'A man-eating lion has escaped from the zoo and is now outside this door trying to get in.' He indicates the door to his office with a casual wave of his pen.

She wants to stop him already. This analogy is just far too illogical. Why did the lion come here? Why this door? It is a hell of a long way from the zoo to here, so how did the lion accomplish the journey without being recaptured or shot? Come to that, how did it manage to get into the building itself—the double doors, the key codes would surely be an obstacle. Can lions manage stairs, or did it take the lift? But she bites her tongue and allows him to continue, she does not want to spoil his fun.

'You and I would have the same choice of responses,' he says assuredly. 'Fight, which I would not advise; flight; or stay like a rabbit caught in the headlights. Hopefully, we would choose flight and we would both be out of that window!'

He motions towards the small window set high in the wall behind him and smiles benignly. She thinks, *'It's a deer caught in the headlights not a rabbit, and neither of us would fit through that window—that is assuming that we managed to reach it.'* She also thinks that maybe flight would not be her option, maybe instead she would stay and attempt to bond with the lion. She likes cats, and a lion is just a bigger version of one after all. And if that did not work, it would definitely be an interesting way to go—death by lion, a lion snack. It would also solve the "embrace your anxiety don't embrace your anxiety" conundrum. But instead she just smiles, and she hears herself saying yes, of course, I'd definitely go out of the window.

He glances at his watch.

'Well, that's us finished for this session,' he smiles. 'Same time next week?'

She nods in confirmation.

'Good. Don't forget to try the experiment,' he says as he escorts her to the door. 'Let's get rid of the crucifixes!'

Thoughts

You have everything. You can be anything. Stop focusing on the negatives. I want you to look in the mirror every day and say "I am gorgeous, I am clever, I am sexy". That is what he tells me.

But I am on the periphery of his life. We can never be anything.

No, you are not! And you never know. Things can change. Who knows what the future holds? Then he says that he loves me.

But it still feels wrong, wanting you, needing you. But you also feel like part of me now. I can't imagine you not being in my life. I feel lost without you.

I can't wait to see you again. I want to see your gorgeous face, your beautiful eyes. I want to kiss you. I need to make sure that you're not a figment of my imagination.

I want you.

I want you too.

The Patient

The first thing that she notices is the change in his attire: peach shirt, blue slacks and a navy raincoat draped over the back of his chair replacing his usual beige linen blazer. He seems restless today, less focused, as if he would rather

be somewhere else. Is she mistaken or did he just close his eyes whilst she was talking to him?

As well as the new jacket he also has a new analogy for her. Today's analogy is about boxes of chocolate on a conveyor belt. The boxes of chocolates represent happy thoughts and memories, but sometimes, instead of chocolates the boxes contain something nasty and unpleasant—these contents symbolise bad memories and upsetting thoughts. The conveyor belt represents her mind, and it is, at present, apparently a little faulty as it keeps getting stuck at a box full of horrible memories and nasty thoughts as opposed to the chocolate filled happy box. She nods, not really paying attention. Her mind is now completely distracted by the thought of chocolate—chocolate covered fudge, strawberry fondant encased in bitter dark chocolate, praline, smooth caramel in milk chocolate, all wrapped up in pretty, shiny, coloured paper. She forces herself to concentrate, to tune her mind back to his words. She focuses back in on his voice to find that seemingly, she needs to compartmentalise these negative thoughts and memories so that her conveyor belt can get moving again thus allowing herself access to the boxes of chocolates—the positive thoughts and memories. This regains her full attention: hasn't he been saying all along that she should confront her negative thoughts? To stop avoiding them? Now he wants her to compartmentalise them. She is confused and irritated once more.

'So, what do you think?' he asks. 'Remember, it's all about you.'

She pauses and then takes a deep breath before plunging in quickly before she loses her confidence and lapses back into obedient silence and acquiescence.

'You're saying that I should compartmentalise bad things and negative things. That's what I've always done, locked them away in a box up here,' she taps her temple with the forefinger of her right hand. 'But you told me before that that was wrong, that it was unhealthy. You said that I should face all those negative thoughts and feelings, all the bad memories. That I had to learn to live with them. But now you're saying the exact opposite, you want me to lock them all away again. What is it that I'm supposed to do?'

He looks momentarily startled and confused by this sudden outpouring of thoughts. He is put off-balance.

'Let me explain,' he says. 'I am not telling you to compartmentalise, but sometimes it is helpful.' He falters and hesitates briefly. 'You need to confront and accept the negatives, the past traumas, and once you have done that—then you can compartmentalise.'

They are both silent for a few minutes. She has run out of words, and she really cannot see the point in arguing or discussing anything with him.

'Let me try another analogy,' he says finally. 'If you were stuck in quicksand, your natural response would be to struggle, but that is exactly what you shouldn't do because the more that you struggle the more you will sink. The only option for survival is to lay down and to spread out your weight. That way you won't sink. It is the only way to survive but it goes against our natural instincts, so it is extremely hard to do. It is the same with bad memories, negative thoughts, and trauma: our natural instinct is to struggle and fight against them. Maybe you— we all—need to consider confronting these negative thoughts and feelings, these traumatic memories. We need to lay down if you like, just as we would need to do with the quicksand, and accept them for what they are. Once that is done, then they can be compartmentalised, and we can move on with our lives in a healthier fashion. We might find that we can survive that confrontation, that we can come through to the other side more effectively than if we continually struggle, if we fight—because that route might overwhelm us.'

Finally she feels that he is beginning to make some sense, even if he still being maddeningly contradictory. He pauses before resuming.

'Remember, there are a lot of doors for you to choose to go through. I'm here to help you find the right one.'

He smiles compassionately and she waits for him to continue, not certain as to how she should respond to yet another analogy.

'So!' he says emphatically, marking a move away from analogies onto slightly firmer ground. 'I feel that there is something bubbling under the surface. We need to explore that. How has your week been?'

'Not good,' she admits. 'The voice is back.'

'And what does this voice say?' he asks.

She sighs and closes her eyes before continuing.

'That I should kill myself. I found myself holding a knife to my wrist,' her voice trails away. 'But it's stupid because I don't think that I really want to die. I just want it all to stop, I want some peace. I've had enough. Life feels like a form of punishment. I just don't like being me.'

'And who is this voice?' he asks gently. 'It doesn't sound like you.'

She shrugs her shoulders. Her eyes are open now, but she can't look at him.

'In your formulation,' he taps the file on his lap, 'I hear words like "worthless", "I don't like me". Subservience. You act as if you are a victim. We

need to change your mindset through realistic thinking. What you went through as a child—and I know you don't feel ready to talk about that yet—that was awful, and no one will ever deny that. And yet here you are a strong woman, a wife, a mother. You are not a victim—you are a survivor.'

He produces a sheet of paper from the file: it is a list of cognitive errors—or black and white thinking—ten in total. She is to read them and tick the ones that apply to her. Glancing through them, seven immediately attract her attention as something that she does if not always, then definitely some of the time. The seven cognitive errors on the list that call to her read: Labelling—judging and defining oneself or others based on an isolated event. Over-generalisation—interpreting one isolated current situation as a sequence of events by using words like "always", "never", when you think about it; in other words an isolated negative event becomes a continual cycle of loss and defeat. Filtering or selective abstraction—focusing on isolated, negative detail and selectively attending to it so that ultimately your interpretation of everything that is happening becomes distorted. Emotional reasoning—assuming your feelings reflect the way things really are—"I feel guilty so I must have done something wrong", "I feel anxious therefore the situation must be dangerous". "Should" and "Must" statements or imperatives—if things aren't the way you want them to be you feel guilty. Personalisation—believing that you are responsible for events that are completely or partially out of your control. Catastrophising—jumping to the worst possible conclusion all the time. She ticks these seven cognitive errors wondering whether this work will ever be referred to again, or like all his other "homework" it will be filed and ultimately forgotten. It was all just so pointless.

Next, he proffers her a card—more therapy notes to add to her growing bundle. Today she has a self-help task to complete. She is to continue to collect on-going evidence (the word "evidence" has been underlined) that "I will not fall apart or go crazy". Apparently, she is also to have a "new assumption" and this new assumption is "it will be unpleasant and not nice, but I can tolerate anxiety"—more underlining, this time on the word "tolerate"—and "anxiety cannot cause me harm", again with underlining on the word "cannot". At this point, she has to voice her opinions; they have gone over this before. She feels quite incensed now at this smug little man and his superior tone.

'You say that anxiety cannot cause me harm?' she says, her voice shaking slightly. 'How can a panic attack or a derealisation—dissociation—episode, whatever you want to call it, how can that be safe? What if I have an episode

while I'm driving or crossing a busy road? Christ, even if I had one while I was cooking! And God forbid what if I had one while minding a child, a baby? What about when I feel suicidal? What if I have an episode then?'

He smiles but he can see that she has flustered him again.

'Have any bad things happened when you are having an episode?' he asks.

'No, but—'

'Well then!' he interrupts as if that settles the matter. 'Like I said previously, if panic and anxiety caused harm the human race would not be here today. We would have been wiped out thousands of years ago.'

He looks down at the file on his lap ostensibly to check his notes, but it is obvious that this is simply his way of marking an end to their discussion. After a brief pause while she fumes and he marks time, he continues.

'I want you to self-monitor your thinking and the situations that are triggering your cognitive distractions—we can discuss them next week,' he says firmly. 'I need you to be more Machiavellian: not everyone is out to get you. I want you to be in it to win it.'

XIII
Memory Matters

The Wife

Coitus. Intercourse. Copulation. Making love. Sex. Fucking. Whatever term you chose to use, for her the act had held nothing but fear and disgust for the longest of times. Intimacy went hand in hand with nasty secrets, dirtiness, and self-loathing. It also went hand in hand with the cry for help from her six-year-old self that had been left un-uttered and therefore unanswered.

Five years of pain and torment. She had endured it all in silence. At six, she had not understood this "special secret" that she had been ordered to keep, and although she did not like the games that she was made to play she had liked having a playmate. By the age of ten, the realisation of what was being done to her, of the five years of violation, hit her full force. She felt alone, ashamed, and helpless: a co-conspirator rather than a victim.

Who could she tell? Who could she turn to for help? Not her parents, that was for certain. They would not believe her, and anyway, she did not want to upset them. She was confused and worried that she was in some way to blame. After all, it was only men that abused little girls, wasn't it? Teenage girls certainly did not.

Her beautiful, clever cousin. Wasn't she lucky to receive such attention, such friendship; to have such a role model, such a mentor. She had been just six and her cousin sixteen when the games had begun. She had built a den for herself in her bedroom, draping sheets over the furniture and the bed to create a snug hidey-hole into which she had secreted her pillow and some of her favourite toys: a baby doll, a tea set, a chalk board, and some chalk. Her cousin had arrived for what was to become the first of many weekend visits. They had been left alone. They were cousins, family, so what was the harm?

She can't remember exactly how it had started, only that it did. Her cousin had joined her—uninvited—in the den and suggested that they play schools. Being the younger of the two she was the pupil and her cousin the strict teacher. Pictures of the human body were drawn on the chalk board and she was told the names of each body part, words that she had never heard before, words that were clumsy on her tongue. Scrotum. Testicle. Foreskin. Breast. Nipple. Labia.

giving their only daughter. How sisterly. How kind. And they never thought to open the door, to check on them, to make sure that everything was ok.

At school, the teachers were beginning to worry about this silent nine-year-old. Why wouldn't she speak? Why wouldn't she play with any of her classmates? Why did she sometimes hit other children for no apparent reason? Meetings were held with her parents. Her parents told the teacher that they were sure that it was only a stage that she was going through, and that she had not always been like this—she used to be chatty and full of fun. It was just a phase; she would grow out of it they were certain. Besides, she was an only child after all, so surely it was to be expected that socialising with her peers could prove difficult. But they told the teacher that there was no need to worry on that front— she had a wonderful older cousin who was sure to bring her out of her shell and help her to adjust. So more visits were duly planned, and she could say or do nothing for fear of retaliation, because of terror and shame, and because of love.

She was nine and her cousin nineteen. She was beginning to know now that something really wasn't right, but she was just so scared.

By the age of ten, her cousin sometimes brought a younger friend along when she visited. She would be relieved when this happened because it meant a slight reprieve. Doctors and nurses was often the game of choice, and if she were really lucky all she would have to do is watch as her cousin performed her own unique style of physical examination on a quiet and subservient friend. But more often than not it was her lying prone on the bed, her legs splayed, her knickers discarded. And if she was really unlucky it wasn't her cousin's friend who joined her on the visit, it was her cousin's older boyfriend who was on hand to give a second opinion. Which of course meant a much more thorough and exhaustive examination had to be endured.

For the next year or so, it became the norm for her cousin to stay overnight, and sleep overs became a regular occurrence. On these overnight stays and weekend visits, the torment continued with no reprieve. No matter how tightly she squeezed her eyes shut and curled herself into a protective ball; no matter how hard she wished herself invisible and prayed that nothing would happen; the inevitable always did: her cousin would slip silently into the bed beside her and press her mature, naked body against her own, forcing her tongue into her tightly closed mouth, her hands groping and squeezing her budding breasts. Her knickers would be removed, and she would feel the coarseness of her cousin's

pubic hair against her flesh, feel the jolt as fingers were forced inside her. The nightmare would begin all over again.

Nightmares, hallucinations, and night terrors. Bed-wetting and sleep walking. Itching where her parents said that she should not itch. Five years of fear. Five years of wondering why her parents never asked her what was wrong. Why didn't they realise? Why didn't they make it stop? Why didn't she say something? What was wrong with her?

But it did stop. Eventually. Abruptly. She was eleven years old and had just started high school. She was beginning to understand the gravity of what was being done to her. She confronted her cousin, screamed at her, and placed her hands around her throat, squeezing as hard as she could. Her cousin had simply laughed. But it never happened again.

It had all come flooding back recently, this dirty unspoken secret which she had carried with her for all these years, locked securely—or so she had thought—in the dark recesses of her mind. She had been at the hairdressers and was reading the problem page in one of those trashy women's magazines. A woman had written in saying how she used to inappropriately touch her younger sister and how badly she now felt about this. The agony aunt had replied that the woman need not worry, explaining it all away as normal childhood curiosity and development. According to the agony aunt the little sister had not been harmed in any way: she wrote that it was all part of growing up, and that it was normal. She had wanted to scream. It was not normal. It was sick. It was disgusting. It was abuse. She sat shaking, longing to be able to reach out for comfort and for help. But who could she turn to? There had been no one then and there certainly was no one now. She summoned up the courage and tried talking to her husband, but she had not got very far, not when she saw the look on his face—the fear and the confusion in his eyes. She could not bear to live with his pity and could not risk his disgust. So the subject was quickly changed and had never been mentioned since, but things—sex, intimacy—were never quite the same again.

As for confiding in her now elderly parents, their niece was still very much a part of their lives, of everyone's lives—her own included when family gatherings and celebrations took place. Her parents adored their niece, they cossetted her, bragged about her, worried about her, and continually supported her. Why can't you be more like her, more outgoing and confident? Your poor cousin is having such a difficult time with her children, they are always acting

out. Think of all she did for you through the years! The poor girl needs your support, you should be helping her. Yes. Poor her.

THOUGHTS
Bitch.

XIV
Life Script

Thoughts

Situations that trigger my cognitive distractions, in no particular order: fluorescent light; certain shades of purple; the smell of open fires; autumn; dark evenings; social situations; confrontations; talking on the phone; making decisions; change; therapy; tiredness; certain people; all people; tractors; goodbyes; life; death; everything; nothing.

The Wife

Her hearing had become muffled as if she were under water or her ears were full of cotton wool. Her hands began to tingle and her palms were sweaty. Her sight was the next to be affected, colours were becoming harsher, and everything—everyone—was swimming in and out of focus before slowly receding into the distance.

She had tried to calm herself, to control her breathing, like she had always done. In through the nose and out through the mouth, in through the nose and out through the mouth. But it was of no use, her panic was rising far too quickly. Her heart was beating so hard and so fast she was sure that it would erupt from her chest. She gasped for breath, it felt like she was suffocating.

She tried to focus on her surroundings. She is in a pharmacy, there are displays of bath products, hair dye and over the counter medicine. How many boxes of hair dye are there? What colours can you see? Focus.

She attempted to hold on to rational thoughts, as she had been told. She tells herself over and over again that this is just anxiety, that she has experienced this all before and was fine, but it is of no use. She is drifting out of her reality.

Why is she here? She cannot remember. Thoughts, visions, and fragments of conversation bounce in and out of her mind like an out-of-control ball in a pinball machine. She cannot determine what is real and what is unreal, what has happened and what has not. She doesn't even remember how she got here. She wants to scream but the sound is ensnared in her throat. It is a living nightmare. She wrings her hands convulsively like a modern-day Lady Macbeth.

The girl behind the counter called her name—her monthly prescription was ready—but she was unable to focus on the words, they were just a jumble of sounds echoing around her, and so instead of approaching the counter she stumbled outside and onto the pavement.

The next thing that she was aware of is that she is at home, lying on her bed and staring up at the ceiling. She is shaking and crying uncontrollably, the tears streaking mascara down her pale cheeks, her eyes bloodshot. She does not remember coming home. She does not know what has happened. She can recall car horns, the squealing of brakes, and angry shouts. Has she been outside? Did that happen? She cannot remember. Eventually she falls into a confused and exhausted sleep clutching her pillow to her breast.

The Patient

The piece of paper taped to the door states in bold, black letters that "your counsellor is waiting to see you. Please enter". The door, as usual, is slightly ajar, but he has not come out to welcome her in at the sound of her footsteps, as he has done on every previous session. So instead of entering the room, she perches nervously on the edge of one of the four uncomfortable chairs that line the wall opposite the doorway. She checks her watch. She is early—another five minutes before she is officially due to be here. She can hear him moving around inside the room—papers are being shuffled, there is the gentle click of the computer keyboard, and the creak of a chair as he adjusts his position in it. *'Should she obey the sign and go in,'* she wonders. She makes to stand and then thinks better of it. He must know after all that she is here, and she doesn't want to barge in, to interrupt him in his work.

A few more minutes pass. *'To hell with it,'* she thinks. The sooner that she goes in, the sooner she can leave. She tentatively pushes the door open and peers in, accompanying the movement with a polite—if nervous—cough. He is sat at the computer—a cream shirt today she notes—the screen displaying some kind of a chart in cerulean blue and white. At her cough, he turns quickly, shutting down the computer as he does so.

'Hello! Sit down!' he exclaims. 'Tea? Coffee?'

'No thank you,' she answers reservedly as she sits.

He settles into the chair opposite her, folder on his lap as always, assuming once again his role of wise sage. Today he wants to discuss her "life script". It

is, according to him, the most important document in her life but it is just outside of her awareness and so she does not even know that it exists.

'You have been programmed by your parents,' he explains. 'They taught you how to behave, what to feel, and how to think; and subsequent events have justified this programming. That is why you are on your current path.'

She really is not sure what he is talking about. It all sounds like some kind of plot from a Le Carré novel: maybe she is actually a Russian spy, waiting to be activated and not a pathetic woman with anxiety issues after all.

'But your Life Script,' she can hear the capital letters as he says the words. 'It needs to change.'

He steeples his long fingers, obviously revelling in his feeling of intellectual superiority.

Changing her life script. This amuses her no end. She has to change a script that is outside of her awareness—how the hell is she supposed to achieve that?—whilst he works each week to his own script with little or no deviation, regardless of what input she may give. He continues.

'Your Life Script has been based on past decisions, on past traumatic events, and on your past interpretations of information,' he expounds. 'This has—is—limiting you. You are defining reality to justify your Script.'

He leans back in his chair and smiles an exultant smile. She wonders if he is expecting a response. She understands, maybe even agrees in part, with what he has said, but she is not quite sure how she should respond. Anyway, he is never really that interested in her opinion, preferring the sound of his own voice, his own Script; and so, she chooses to remain silent.

'You have—we all have—our own perceived realities,' he continues. 'And that is not objective. Your reality is based on past traumas and your responses to them. Your thoughts create feelings, your feelings create behaviour, and your behaviour reinforces thoughts. It is an endless cycle.'

He pauses and re-crosses his legs before continuing.

'We need to examine your Life Script, your perceived reality, because it is inhibiting your spontaneity. It is limiting you: stopping you from being the best you can be. Instead of a personal reality, I want you to have some objective truth. Thoughts?'

She looks at him, caught by surprise by his sudden interest in her opinion. Where to start? The life script and personal reality theory makes some sense, as does the cycle of feelings, behaviour and thoughts all influencing and impacting

on each other. But finding objective truth instead of a personal, perceived reality? He had lost her. She had no idea what he was talking about.

'I guess that makes sense,' she murmurs quietly, not wanting to reveal her ignorance and knowing that he likes her in the role of the compliant student.

'Before we continue, let me just emphasise that I am not above you. I am not better than you. I believe—and correct me if I am wrong,' he smirks—as if he could ever be wrong—'That you cast yourself in the role of an inferior. You consider everyone to be above you. You are subservient, a victim—'

'No! Not at all!' she interrupts. 'Sometimes, yes. Maybe. But no…'

He smiles and nods, jotting down something in his notepad.

'I am here to validate you,' he says, his eyes boring into hers. She looks away, focusing on a point just to the left of his oily head.

'You have been through horrible, horrible times. No one is doubting that. They were real,' he says sincerely. 'You do not need to persuade me of that. What is happening now is horrible—wrong. But you cannot change the past. You cannot change other people. You can only change you. You have to stop living in the past and you have to stop having so many regrets. I want you to know that you are of worth, that you are important. Your mindset is one of "I am not worthy", "I am not equal". You let others control you. You haven't been playing the game.'

He pauses, smiling beatifically. She imagines that he is hearing a fanfare of celestial beings or a triumphant soundtrack as he reaches the end of his speech.

'Does that sound correct?' he asks.

'Sorry?' she replies. She has tuned out, trying to guess the sort of music he would like. 'I don't understand.'

'Does that sound like a good goal for the coming weeks?' he attempts to clarify. 'To do things for you. To be more assertive. To put you first.'

'Yes, I suppose so,' she answers uncertainly.

'Excellent!' he exclaims. 'We'll add that to your original goals of coping with depression and managing your panic attacks and derealisation episodes.'

He writes furiously in his notepad before continuing.

'Remember: it doesn't matter if it doesn't work. It is the trying that counts.'

He puts away the notepad and closes the file abruptly before glancing at his watch.

'I'll see you the same time next week.'

XV
Counsel

The Patient

Another day, another waiting room. This one is large with an assortment of chairs lining the white walls. The walls themselves are adorned with shelves containing leaflets concerning various cheerful subjects including how to spot bowel cancer and how to check your breasts for lumps—definitely a running theme here. Various posters and signs are also taped to the walls and pinned to a noticeboard, urging the waiting patients to join a new mums' walking club or a "men's shed", whatever that was. It sounded dubious.

It is ten past eleven by the clock on the far wall. Her appointment was for eleven and she is feeling restless. A middle-aged woman in a black padded jacket is also waiting to be seen. She had no appointment but has demanded one. She is proving to be very adamant. The receptionist says that she will have to wait until everyone else has been dealt with. Dealt with—not seen. An odd choice of words for a mental health clinic. Far too aggressive and ominous in her opinion. But the woman in the black padded jacket does not seem to mind and she sits down. Even seated she is fidgety and her eyes dart nervously around the room, but she has been placated, at least for now.

More of the lost arrive, including a woman in her late fifties, eyes glazed, staring blindly at the wall opposite her. She is accompanied by a man of around the same age. Her husband? Brother? Carer? It is hard to tell as they do not communicate with each other or even acknowledge the others existence. Instead, they simply sit in silence.

Next a young boy arrives, he is maybe fifteen or sixteen years of age. He too has vacant eyes like the older woman, but his demeanour is slightly different as every now and then he appears to resurface from wherever it is he is hiding and becomes aware of his surroundings. '*He shouldn't be here alone,*' she thinks to herself, concerned.

A woman enters the room clasping a file to her ample breast. She is wearing a long floating skirt, her long grey hair loose about her shoulders, her sandals slapping on the floor as she quickly ushers the teenager into her office. He is soon replaced by another boy of about the same age. Like the boy before him, he

also has glazed, vacant eyes, but his eyes occasionally light up in fear, confusion, and agitation. She thinks that the two boys could almost be twins. The second boy has been brought in by his mother judging by her age and the similarity in features, but she too seems a little lost, a little dazed. *'Perhaps insanity is contagious,'* she ponders. The mother is vocal, the usual banal attempts at conversation—the weather, current news. She gets a few nervous smiles in response before everyone finds great fascination in their mobile phones or their laps. Never once does she try to engage her son in conversation. Conversation topics exhausted, the mother—clearly anxious—abruptly stands and leaves the room with no apparent thought for her silent son.

Her name is finally called. *'Thank God,'* she thinks, *'no more avoiding eye contact with the insane and their cohorts.'* The psychiatrist is a small Indian man, young, not much more than thirty years old. He shepherds her into his office, politely holding the door open for her, head bowed, ladies first. The room is large and sparse, with bare white walls. A table, adorned with the requisite file, is in the centre of the room with one chair placed on the side nearest the door and two on the side furthest away. He directs her to sit at one of the chairs on the farthest side of the table, and she nervously sits facing the door. She wonders idly what the reason is for this change in the customary seating arrangements. Is it so the patient feels safer seeing a direct escape route? Or is it so the psychiatrist himself has the easier way out in the event that a patient decides to leap across the table in a frenzied attack? Or more likely it is to make it harder for the patient to leave.

The psychiatrist introduces himself, proffering his hand. He has impeccable manners she notes. Hands are duly shook and he proceeds to glance through her file. She can see a few pages that are stapled together, these pages have boxes to tick and sections to complete. There are also copies of her counselling sessions and correspondence from her doctor.

'So,' he says, looking up from the file. 'Your doctor says that you have been experiencing some difficulties—anxiety attacks and hearing voices?'

His accent is strong, and is quite difficult to understand, but he has kind eyes, and she finds him reassuring.

'Yes,' she replies.

'Can you explain your anxiety please,' he instructs. She pauses and steadies her breath before answering.

'Sometimes I just get breathless, and I feel scared. But sometimes the light changes—it gets harsher—and I can't hear properly. And if I were looking at

you, you would suddenly seem really far away. And I can't work things out—reality from dreams, from memories. I don't know what I'm doing, where I am, who I am…' she trails off, exhausted by such a long and revealing speech.

He jots down two words: "derealisation" and "dissociation". She is amazed: a doctor with legible handwriting.

'How often do you have these attacks?' he asks looking up briefly from his notes.

'I've had them ever since I was a child. The slight one I have every now and then,' she replies. 'The worse one, maybe every couple of weeks. It depends.'

'And how long does the worse one last?' he asks as he continues to write.

'A couple of hours normally,' she says. 'But last week I had one that was virtually the whole week—not full blown, just simmering.'

'And what do you do when you have these attacks?' he asks, making eye contact for a moment.

'I try to focus on my breathing and on my surroundings,' she replies. 'They scare me, the attacks. I just want them to stop. My counsellor suggested that I should focus on them, that stopping them is avoidance. He says that they're nothing to be scared of.'

He looks up abruptly from his notes, his face is suddenly quite stern, and his eyes bore into hers.

'Oh no,' he says firmly. 'They are definitely something to be concerned about and they are very scary, and they can be extremely dangerous. Never focus on them. You need to turn to someone for support and encouragement—your husband, a friend—or go to places that you find calm and comforting.'

She is reassured. The usual questions then follow: childhood? Not perfect but on the whole good. Your parents? Ditto. Home life? Fine. Alcohol? On occasion. Drugs? Never. And so on and so on.

'And any sexual abuse in your childhood?' he queries poring over her file.

She pauses, unsure as to what to say, whether she should risk opening up.

'Well, yes. When I was a child, I was sexually abused for a few years,' she finally concedes. 'But I'm not ready to talk about that yet.'

'That's fine, that's fine,' he says smiling kindly. 'We'll come back to that in a few weeks.'

Is she mistaken or is he looking very relieved?

'Now,' he continues. 'These voices that your doctor mentions that you've been hearing, what are they saying?'

'That I'm useless. That I should die,' she murmurs.

'Is it one voice or many?' he queries.

'One,' she replies.

'Who do you think it is?' he asks.

'Me,' she answers definitively before becoming less certain. 'It's just me I think. My subconscious. Isn't it? We all talk to that voice up here, don't we? Our secret self.' She taps the side of her head and then continues to speak more decisively. 'It's just me and I try to discuss things or to tell myself "no".'

'So, no hallucinations?' he prods.

'No. Just me. It's just me talking,' she answers.

'And you can control them, these conversations?' he probes.

'I guess,' she says hesitantly.

'And self-harm? These suicidal thoughts?' he persists.

'I don't want to die, not really' she responds, finding it hard to put her thoughts and feelings into words. 'I just want it all to stop. To end. I've had enough of this feeling of uselessness, of hopelessness. There's really little point in anything, is there? It's all too much.'

'But have you self-harmed or thought of self-harming?' he presses.

'Yes. I've held a knife to my wrist. I tried to hang myself.' With this last statement, she becomes more animated and almost cheerful. 'That was nice in a way. When I made the decision to hang myself, when I had the cord around my neck, I felt so calm and finally in control. It felt right. I want to feel like that all the time.' She pauses and the good mood ebbs away and she is downcast once more. 'But I stopped myself. I always manage to stop myself.'

He puts his notepad and pen down on the table and leans forward.

'Promise me that you won't do this again,' he says earnestly, fiercely. 'I see this every day, day in and day out, and all it will do is cause pain to others. All you are doing is passing your suffering on to someone else, to someone that you love. Do you understand? Do you want someone that you love to feel the way you are feeling?'

She shakes her head, her eyes, which are now filling with tears, are gazing unseeing at her hands in her lap. She feels ashamed and useless. She never can get anything right.

'People care about you. I care about you,' he continues more gently. 'So please, no more thoughts about this.'

He picks up his notepad and pen and resumes writing before continuing to speak.

'And how are you sleeping?' he asks, all business once more.

'Not well, despite the sleeping tablets. I have bad dreams and I wake up exhausted,' she responds, stifling her tears.

'Nightmares?' he queries.

'No, not really,' she answers. 'Just dreams that make me feel worried—I'll be lost, or I'll be trying to get away from some threat or other, or my home will be taken. That kind of thing.'

He glances at his notes for a few minutes.

'So, it would be fair to say that you are feeling under enormous stress, that you are suffering panic attacks, you are hearing voices, not sleeping and having suicidal thoughts.' It is not a question but rather a statement, but she nods, nonetheless.

'Ok,' he says assertively. 'I have to write a few things up and talk to my colleague. If you'd like to go back to the waiting room and I'll call you in a few minutes.'

*

Fifteen minutes later and she is back in the room. The psychiatrist has an appointment card for her: she is now officially under the protection and guidance of the mental health unit.

'So,' he says. 'I have spoken to my colleague, and we are in agreement that you are exhibiting signs of post-traumatic stress disorder and depression. You will come back to me in three months' time. I will also put you on the waiting list to see our psychologist for cognitive behavioural therapy.'

'Oh,' she interjects. 'I'm already doing that with my counsellor. I'm doing an eight-week course of cognitive behavioural therapy with him.'

'Really?' He appears confused.

'Yes,' she responds. 'My counsellor—therapist—I'm not sure what to call him—well he says that I have to put myself first and be assertive. He's the one who said that I have to stop avoiding my panic attacks and to immerse myself in them instead.'

He suddenly laughs and she notices that his teeth are small, like little milky baby teeth, with gaps between each one. He catches himself and regains his composure before continuing.

'Please, never immerse yourself in a panic attack,' he says, serious once more. 'It is like I said before, that is a dangerous thing to do. Do your breathing, try meditation, turn to a friend, go for a walk. Do whatever calms you.'

'Thank you,' she says, relieved once more at this repeated advice. 'That makes more sense to me. Not that everything he says doesn't,' she adds, feeling a sudden disloyalty, a betrayal.

'If you were a dependent sort of person, then maybe we would suggest avoiding certain situations and certain behaviours,' he pronounces. 'Anyway, I'll put you on our cognitive behaviour therapy waiting list. It will be a while before you get an appointment—a couple of months at least—but it will be much better, I am sure.'

'Ok,' she replies.

'We will also change your medication,' he says authoritatively. 'Your anti-depressant will increase to fifteen milligrams for a week and after that to twenty milligrams—''For how long?' she interjects, unnerved. 'I don't want to keep taking medicine. I don't want to become reliant on it.'

'For six to nine months only. We have to increase your serotonin levels and in conjunction with cognitive behavioural therapy—with techniques like mindfulness—we can help you,' he clarifies.

'Ok,' she feels reassured but only slightly.

'Also,' he continues. 'We will put you on a low dose of pregabalin for three months.'

'No,' she says firmly. 'I've heard of that and I know what it can do. I am not taking that.'

'Just for three months,' he soothes.

'No!' She is adamant. 'I will not take it! I told you. I know what it does. Dizziness, blurred vision, confusion, delusions, memory loss. I don't want to get addicted or to become a zombie like the rest of your patients! I've seen them out there in the waiting room!'

'Only for three months, it will only be a low dose and we will be monitoring you,' he attempts to placate. 'Not everyone gets addicted and not everyone has issues whilst on this drug.'

'I'll take something else,' she responds firmly. Being seen every three months was not monitoring.

'No, pregabalin,' he says inflexibly, refusing to be swayed by her fears. 'I understand your concerns, but…' He trails off.

'I do not want to take it!' Her voice is raised now, and she is beginning to feel a tightness in her chest.

'For a week then?' he appeases. 'See how it goes?'

'No, I told you!'

'Just for a week and we will monitor you,' he perseveres. 'Any sign of an issue and you can stop taking it.'

She senses she will not win this argument and, exhausted, she concedes.

'Ok,' she mumbles.

'Good!' he replies, relieved. 'We will see you back here in three months, and in the meantime, any problems—if you feel overwhelmed—call this number,' he underlines a telephone number on the appointment card. 'We are here Monday to Friday, nine to five.'

She wonders what she is supposed to do out of office hours or on weekends. Maybe you're not allowed to be unwell or suicidal during these periods.

*

At her doctor's surgery a little while later, she cautiously hands her new appointment card which lists her new prescription, to the receptionist. She feels awkward and embarrassed, now everyone knows that she is mentally unstable. The card made it too real, she was officially insane.

'I need these prescriptions please,' she says. 'But not the pregabalin. I'm not taking that.'

The Woman

Hey you.

Hey you.

All good?

Yes. Are you ok? Did you start taking the new pills?

Yes.

I thought so. I can see your mood swings a lot. Is it because of the pills?

No. it's just me. You can empathise with him now having to put up with my mood swings!

Sorry in advance, but I will never empathise with that prick. If you ever want to talk to me, don't ever call him sweet names and don't ever tell me he's a good man. He is just a kidnapper. He's holding you hostage and you are too weak to do anything about it. I pray to God that one day you will have the power to stand up for yourself.

He loves me—flaws and mood swings too—and I don't see anyone else lining up to do that. And for the record I am not weak.

For sure, Stockholm Syndrome.

XVI
A Voice and Nothing More

The Patient

'Hi! I wasn't expecting to see you today,' he says, obviously taken by surprise. 'I only have about five minutes to spare before my next client. Are you ok? I was worried about you when you missed last week's session, in fact I was just about to give you a call.'

There is an awkward pause while he considers what to say next and how to get her out of his office before his next appointment. He is lying about the phone call claim, she knows this. Suddenly tears begin to fill her eyes and her body begins to tremble.

'I'm scared, I don't know what I'm supposed to do,' she sobs. 'The voice, it won't stop.'

'It's ok, try and stay calm,' he reaches for her to comfort her but quickly changes his mind, it would be inappropriate and unprofessional, and he lets his arms fall limply to his sides. He gathers his thoughts swiftly and continues in a more business-like fashion. 'I have a formulation for you, a hypothesis: you are not going mad, you are not schizophrenic, and you are not bi-polar. It is just an inner voice, inner conversations.'

He is more confident now that he is back to a script that feels safe.

'This inner voice was caused by past trauma,' he continues. 'It has re-emerged due to this present and very real problem that you are currently encountering in your marriage.'

She nods her head imperceptibly and wipes her eyes and nose roughly with the back of her hand.

'We can talk more in our next counselling session. Ok? Try and stay calm,' he continues to talk and as he does so, he edges her closer and closer to the door, guiding her gently, his hand on her elbow.

'I really have to see my next client. Relax and enjoy your weekend. I'll see you Monday.'

And with his last words the door is closed on her.

Thoughts

It's time to die now please. Kill yourself. No one cares, not really—not enough. They're just pretending. Playing the game.

You are a stupid bitch. What a waste of space. You're no good. Useless. You need to die. It's time. You won't be missed.

The Woman

I wonder how much alcohol and tablets I'd need to escape.
You just need to keep doing as you are told. Obey your orders like a good girl.
I'm being serious. It's not funny.
You're not funny. If you don't like where you are, move. You're not a tree.
Fine. Blah blah blah.
Your life is blah blah blah, but you like it. You are a submissive woman indeed.
I don't like it. You think I'm joking when I talk about ending things. Why do you think I have counselling sessions? Why do you think the doctor put me on these tablets?
Ending what things?
Everything.
Are you stupid? I'd slap you right now if I were there. Can I ring you?
It's just all so pointless. Please just enjoy your weekend. I shouldn't have contacted you. Its ok. I won't do anything stupid.
Please be ok. I'm here for you anytime. Except when you're annoying! See you next week?
I've just had enough.
Monday? Tuesday?
I'm fed up being sad and scared.
Move in with me then.
Very funny.
Right.
I love you.
Love you too.

The Wife

She remembers the day in minutiae. Her thoughts had been astoundingly clear. She had felt more rational and more in control than she had ever been in

160

her entire life. It was a truly wonderful feeling. She had suddenly possessed such clarity and so much confidence. This was the right thing to do. She had taken the thick cord from her dressing gown and tied it securely to the rail in the heavy oak wardrobe. She remembers giving it a few perfunctory tugs to ensure that it would hold. Then she had turned and faced the window through which the warm summer sun shone. A soft breeze had billowed the lace curtains inwards, and she could hear the liquid song of a blackbird and the sound of small children playing. It was perfect. She had known with absolute certainty that this was what she had to do, that this was what was needed to be done. There was no alternative, no other way out. This simple act would save them all.

Sweeping her long hair out of the way, she had carefully tied the other end of the cord around her neck. Two knots. Nothing fancy, but they were secure. They would hold. She pulled the cord tight and immediately she had felt the constriction in her throat, and she found it harder to breathe, for the air to reach her lungs. But she didn't panic. It felt strangely pleasant: she finally felt in control.

She leant forward, further and further, the cord tightening behind her. Her neck, her face, burned; her eyes bulged; but still she leant farther forward embracing the pain as her own. She remembers trying to focus on the floor, attempting to contemplate the intricate patterns in the wood. She must remember to give it a good scrub another day. The mundanity and stupidity of this thought had hit her like a slap across the face. She was going to die, and she hadn't washed the floor.

She began to scrabble frantically at the cord around her neck, pulling feebly at the knots. Finally, it had loosened, and she fell forward onto the floor, gasping for air. Sobs began to convulse her body and it felt as if slivers of glass were sliding and scraping down her throat. She had failed. She couldn't even kill herself. She felt the fear wash over her, consuming her, and then the voices began again, relentless and taunting. They would never stop.

XVII
A Memory Affair

The Girl

25 October

Dear Diary,

I don't know what to do. I thought that everything was ok. Things have been great between us for a long time now. We have been married four years and we have our own place. We have no real money worries. And I love being a full-time mum, I always have. But I've met someone else.

Why shouldn't I have more than one partner, have feelings for more than one person? There isn't just that one special person out there waiting—there are many. Why shouldn't I grab happiness when and where I can? Life is too short not to live in the moment.

I don't think that it's love. But it is incredibly special—it's that need to feel, to be wanted.

I need him. I need them both.

I'm so confused.

X

The Woman

Hey you. I just wanted to remind you how much you mean to me and how much I miss you. I'm feeling romantic today. I'm also feeling horny. Where are you when I need you?

Thank you. Hopefully one day.

I'm counting on it.

I will sort out a day. I'll get the ropes and blindfolds ready.

Good. You know I need you right?

I need details.

As in I feel like I have two partners. As in I miss talking to you. And to put it bluntly I really want to fuck you.

I feel the same.

That's good.

Can I ask you something? If it were possible, would you like to have us both at the same time?

You really like taking me out of my comfort zone, don't you? I'm blushing!

I meant just theoretically, if he was ok with it. Would it be a fantasy of yours?

It would be a fantasy of mine, yes.

Now I'm horny as well.

*

Happy Valentine's Day! Any romantic stuff for me?

I'm not the romantic type, I have no time for that.

Well, I am, and I do. You know, when I first met you, you turned my world upside down. I never thought that I was capable of feeling the way that I do, I never dared to think or hope that you might feel the same. I did everything that I could to spend time with you, my heart ached for you, and I decided to throw caution to the wind and let you know how I felt. I fell in love with you and along with all the good feelings it can also make me sad, jealous, upset, guilty, and confused. I love you, and it's ok—I know that you really love her and not me, and I would never do anything to hurt either of you—but I will never stop loving you.

Wow. Most amazing love letter I got in years. Love you back.

Thoughts

Where is my ass picture? You should know that I want a picture every day. I can't wait to spank you. I love your ass. I'd love a picture with your legs spread, I would come so much. I want to choke you and slap you. I'm so hard right now.

This is what he tells me. And they say romance is dead.

I climb on top of him. I am naked. I kiss his lips, his neck, his chest. I tell him that I want to kiss women—to touch them, to feel our skins together, to slip my tongue inside her soft mouth and to caress her voluptuous breasts. He can watch us, he can join in. But he says that I am enough for him, that he doesn't want anyone else. He's no fun today.

I move slowly lower down until I reach his cock. I lick it up and down, up and down. I gently caress the tip with my tongue, tasting the saltiness. I kiss it: gentle butterfly kisses. Then I put it in my mouth and suck hard.

I pause. Do you want to come in my mouth? Or inside me? Or both?

He wants both.

He's inside me now, hard and powerful. I don't want him though. I want someone else. I want another man inside me, I want to feel his hardness, his body. It's been too long. I miss him. It's no threat. They can both fuck me—one in the ass and one in the mouth. They can take turns. Sharing is caring after all, and I have enough love for them both.

He says he'll fuck me and I can suck the other man off. I don't believe him. It's just fantasy.

He said: the more I know your kinky side, the more I want you. I really want to fuck your ass the next time I see you. Can I do that? And I want to slap you really hard. I'm still playing with myself thinking of you. I really want to see you sucking dick. I want kids, so make me one.

This is what he said to me. He offered me cake—cream and chocolate—and he gently wiped the stray crumbs from my mouth. He leant forward and moved my hair behind my ears. His hands were soft, almost feminine. When I teased him about that, he playfully slapped my cheek. He said why couldn't I have found you first.

When I went to leave, he said that he wasn't finished with me. We kissed passionately, his tongue hard and forceful. He held my head in both his hands then twined my hair with one hand to pull me into him again. He kissed my neck and sent shivers down my spine. He pinched my nipples and sucked them.

I slipped my hand inside his trousers, inside his pants, and I caressed his large, hard cock. My hand was warm and wet.

But I had to go.

I tried to leave but as I turned he pulled me into him again. My body fits perfectly into his strong chest. I could feel the hard, throbbing thrust of his penis. He kissed my neck again.

I have to go.

Go on then. Go.

The Woman

I wonder how long it will be before I am able to see you again. The universe is acting against me.

It's you who controls the universe.

I didn't know I had that much power.

167

I know you didn't, but you do. When you say things like "I can't", then you better know that that's not true. Nothing is impossible.

You're very philosophical today.

I'm having a holistic approach towards life.

I wish I could. I'm pissed off with everything.

Well, if you don't like it, do something.

It's not that easy. I keep making plans and nothing goes right. For example: I had to cancel coming to see you today. Everything goes wrong. I'm always alone.

You've been practicing being a victim for a lifetime.

I know. I'm an expert at it. I promise I'll see you soon.

Right.

Do I detect disbelief?

I'm losing faith.

Don't. you can't get rid of me that easily. I'll see you soon.

*

I spent all last night over-analysing and over thinking everything that we've ever said to each other.

And? Any conclusion?

I'm addicted to you.

Very funny. Hardly. So, did you think about what I said before about a threesome? Me, you, and her?

I have thought about it. Maybe. But be honest, if I did would you then say goodbye for good? Like you did with the other women you had threesomes with?

Why would I?

I just figured that you would…

God. Your mind! Really? You're already jumping to what's after.

That's me. I like to know where I stand.

Not where you think you do.

Very cryptic. Plain English please.

Plain English: why would you compare yourself with other women? I told you, they were just sex, and it was only a few times. What do you want, a contract?

No. I was just wondering. You know me, I over think.

I don't even know what to say.

That's fine. At the moment, you have a definite maybe. I just need confidence.

I don't even know what a definite maybe is. And how would you get confidence?

God knows. I do want to though.

I don't think that we speak the same language today. What do you mean?

As in I want to sleep with you again.

I knew that!

Ok. And you want a threesome and I kind of do too but I'm nervous. I've never done that sort of thing before.

Of course you're nervous. I am as well. But that's only normal.

Ok.

Any more what ifs?

Of course! Do you know me at all?

Thoughts

He wants to see pictures and videos of the kinkiest things I've ever done. It would be a turn-on for him to see me being dominant: sitting on his face and making him eat me out, me playing hard with his cock and his balls. Some slapping, maybe some ass spanking. He says I should only allow him a certain amount of time to fuck me and that he has to come before the time is up. I am to control his dick and his head.

He says that the biggest turn-on would be for me to be in total control of the relationship, for me to be able to tell him that I'm going to fuck both of them. He has to wait for me to finish fucking him and when I get home, then it will be his turn. He can eat me up. One man for dinner and another man for dessert.

He says I should whisper in his ear that I want to fuck another man and that I want him to watch. He'll get so hard he'll start asking me—begging me—for these types of games.

Dominate him. Try to be in control. Get him to eat you. Tell him how to do it. Tell him how you like it. Faster. Harder.

Wouldn't you like to be fucked by both of them?

Don't you want to be more confident, more powerful?

XVIII
Ifs and Buts

The Lover

She rings the doorbell and waits anxiously for what seems like an eternity for him to answer the door. Once again, she wonders if he has forgotten their arrangement. Should she go now or keep ringing the doorbell? She starts to leave and as she crosses the road, she hears his voice.

'Where are you going?' he calls.

'I thought you must be out,' she answers retracing her steps.

'Why would I be out when we arranged to meet?' he replies amused and a little annoyed with her.

He is dressed casually in shorts and a T shirt; his tousled hair is damp. He must have been in the shower. He obviously prefers clean sex. The irony. He pulls her to him and kisses her forcefully, their tongues exploring. He is rough, urgent. He grabs her face, and then he explores her body, fondling her breasts, and slapping her buttocks.

'So, what do you want?' he asks huskily as he half drags her up the stairs.

'You,' she replies.

He opens the door to the bedroom and once safely inside they continue to kiss, to grab, to explore each other frantically, as if this moment might never happen again. She sits on the edge of the bed and takes of her top, her bra, her shoes; and when she looks up, he is there before her, naked and resplendent. He is tall, lean, and muscular, in perfect proportion all except for his penis which is huge and firm. He leans down and sucks and bites at her nipples. She gasps, enjoying the pleasure that comes with the pain, then watches in anticipation of what is to come as he holds his erect penis and rubs it, moving his hand backwards and forwards. Suddenly he pushes it into her mouth, and she sucks at it hungrily, nipping and licking its soft, salty tip whilst caressing his balls with her hand. He is so big she almost chokes.

He pulls he to her feet and kisses her gently before asking once more if he can take her from behind. Of course he can, although she would prefer the intimacy of seeing his face. But she does not say this to him, she is his to do as he pleases. She kneels on the bed, and he positions her according to his desires.

He murmurs softly in her ear, "feel your pussy". Her hand moves down obediently. She is wet and tender. She wants him so much it is almost unbearable. He slips inside her. He slaps her and moves faster and harder. She cries and moans in pleasure, but he is still not fast enough, and she needs to feel more. There is not enough pain. There is just not enough. And then he shouts in ecstasy, pulls out and comes, and she is left naked and gasping on the bed, needing more.

The Woman

Hey, how are things?

Look, I'm busy. We'll talk another time.

I thought that you liked talking to me.

I do, but it's only when you can escape for a few minutes. When I want to talk to you, you're not there. I only hear from you every now and then. I barely ever see you. It's not a fair trade. I'm here for you all the time but you're not the same for me.

I am here now. You know that it's difficult for me. I know you're there for me and I do try to be there for you too. I want to be here for you.

You have to understand, I feel like Aladdin's lamp sometimes—stuck inside, hidden, only released when you need me. Where is this going anyway?

You're right. I'm sorry.

Don't be sorry, just try to understand my feelings as well. I have been open and honest with you right from the start.

I do understand. I stay in contact with you because I want to feel part of your life and you of mine, even if only in a small way. I'm sorry if that's selfish.

It is selfish and you know that. I'm just someone—something—that you use, that you turn on and off whenever you like or whenever you're allowed.

I am in love with you. I am in love with him. I want you both in my life. I need you both in my life.

The only problem is we both know that, but he doesn't.

If I tell him, I would lose everything.

I know that. I can't tell you what to do but you need to change something if you want anything to do with me.

I know.

I am not ok with leftovers, and I need someone independent beside me, not someone who is needy. You can be that person. It's up to you. It's so sad to see

all that potential going to waste—and maybe it's the same for me too. So anyway, a few things need to change.

Ok. Sorry.

No need to apologise. I want what is best for you. I hope you find a way to be the best version of you.

The best version of me includes you. I love you.

Love you too.

Thoughts

I can't wait to see you again. I need to make sure that you are not a figment of my imagination. I want to see your gorgeous deep brown eyes, to run my fingers through your hair, to feel your stubble against my cheek. I want to count the freckles on your arms, to trace your tattoos, to feel your soft hands on my skin, to see you smile that mischievous smile.

I touch myself thinking of you. I come whispering your name.

The Lover

He meets her at the door, his large penis erect, and pulls her inside, kissing her and pinching her firm nipples. He slips her top over her head and unclasps her bra. He says he has some surprises for her, but he won't tell her what they are no matter how hard she begs him to. They wouldn't be a surprise then, would they?

He takes her upstairs and lies her gently on the bed and they kiss ardently, their hands exploring each other's naked bodies. His fingers slip in and out of her, alternately caressing and slapping. She is wet with excitement. He produces one of his surprises: a large vibrator which he positions between her thighs, ordering her not to remove it. She moans and arches her back in a frenzy of rapture. The other surprise—a camera secreted in the room and filming their every move—he may or may not disclose. He has not decided yet.

'Are you my slut?' he asks gruffly. 'Do you love me?'

She murmurs her assent to both of these questions, transported by her feelings of bliss. He rolls her onto her stomach, making sure the vibrator is still in place, and begins to sensually rub oils onto her buttocks. The pleasure that she feels is indescribable, it verges on pain. It is almost too much to bear, and she feels lightheaded as if at any moment she may lose consciousness. Then there is more agonising pleasure as he slips a jewelled butt plug inside her—another of

his surprises. Now she is on her knees, the vibrator forgotten. As he takes her from behind, he tells her that she is beautiful. He moves faster and faster, harder and harder, slapping her over and over.

'Hurt me!' she screams.

Afterwards they lie exhausted and glistening with sweat side by side on the bed. His head is buried face down in the rumpled bed sheets and she surveys his long, lean, muscular body with satisfied delight. Her love for him is almost all-consuming. He lifts his head and meets her gaze.

'Feel my heart,' he says breathlessly, a smile playing on his lips. 'It's beating so fast, I'm dying.'

She places a hand on his chest and then runs her fingers through his hair before leaning in to kiss him. In turn, his hand traces the curves of her body until he finds her, still moist. He slips his hand between her thighs and thrusts his fingers inside her.

'My slut,' he murmurs.

The Woman

Hey, how are things?

All good. Don't contact me anymore.

Why?

There's no point.

There's no point in anything really, except having you in my life.

But you don't have me in your life. So what's the point?

I'm doing my best. I want to see you.

Don't. I said there's no point. We're just going round in circles.

You're breaking my heart.

You're wasting my time.

I don't know what to say.

There's nothing to say. Live your life and stop fantasising about me and what could be and never will be. It's pointless.

I still love you.

I don't want to block you. Leave me alone.

The Patient

Her new cognitive behavioural therapist had been assigned to her by the mental health unit to help her to develop coping strategies to address some issues

relating to her anxiety. The therapist was waiting for her on the steps of the imposing Victorian building in which her weekly sessions were to take place. A small, middle-aged woman with fiery red hair, wearing leggings and a floral blouse, the therapist proceeded to guide her through the labyrinthine corridors—corridors obviously designed to confuse and disorientate the former patients that were once incarcerated here. As she followed her guide, her flaming hair like a beacon in the gloom, she mused as to what the former patients may have been institutionalised for. Throughout history women had been declared lunatic for a plethora of ridiculous reasons: masturbation, abusive language, political excitement (surely a contradiction in terms), over exertion, drinking, laziness, childbirth, grief, having an opinion, love, religion, domestic troubles, smoking, bad company, sex before marriage, the menopause. The list was endless. She would be locked up for life if that criteria still applied today. And she would have been subjected to what? Not talking therapy that's for sure. No, she would have been restrained in a strait jacket or chained with her hands under her knees, not allowed to stand up. She might have been put in an insulin induced coma or had electric shock treatment—the latter she was almost certain still occurred in America. Worse still a lobotomy might have been performed. And she thought that she had it bad with anti-depressants and cognitive behavioural therapy.

She continued to walk through the maze of corridors as she pondered the fate of all those lost souls. The corridors were dark and full of shadows, she half expected a minotaur to leap out at her from around every corner or at the very least to find a table with a vial set upon it labelled "drink me". The vial would contain pregabalin no doubt. Instead, she eventually found herself seated in yet another sterile box of a room, the obligatory manilla file placed on the desk between herself and the therapist.

'So,' the therapist said. 'As you are aware I work as a cognitive behavioural therapist, and I want to discuss how CBT can help you. Today I just want to quickly review your previous cognitive behavioural therapy sessions in conjunction with your psychiatric notes so that we can make a plan of action.'

She pauses and looks for all the world like a cross school ma'am or a disappointed mother, and then continues tersely.

'You can't go on indefinitely with cognitive behavioural therapy you know. You have to become your own therapist. Not that I'm trying to get rid of you of course.' She laughs nervously.

'Of course not, I understand,' she replies. She does understand—they are fed up with her already, they no longer want to help.

'What we—you—need,' the therapist continues, 'is a clearly defined goal, otherwise there really is no point in us continuing.'

'Ok,' she responds. Yes, there is the confirmation: they do want rid of her.

'Cognitive behavioural therapy can help you manage your problems by changing the way that you think and behave,' the therapist explains.

There is a brief pause.

'So, what are you hoping to achieve here?' the therapist demands. 'What needs to change?'

She is momentarily disconcerted. She wasn't expecting such a direct approach, not so quickly anyway.

'I'm not sure. I know that I need to be more assertive and more in control. But that's really something that only I can do, isn't it?' So much for assertiveness.

'Yes, but we can help you with that,' the therapist replies. 'There are courses on emotional regulation that I can refer you to, and we can also work on some meditation techniques that will help to calm both your mind and your body.'

The therapist looks on quizzically, an eyebrow half raised. She is expecting more from her.

'That sounds good I guess,' she says. 'I want to manage my emotions better—my mood swings. They're just too much. I'm either really happy or really down—there's no in-between. And when I'm really happy I can't even enjoy that feeling because I know that I'm going to crash, to hit rock bottom, at any minute. And when I do crash, I just stop everything—relationships, work, projects—everything. It all just gets side-lined, put on the back burner, forgotten, even though when I was in that good mood I had so many ideas and plans, so much already achieved...' she trails off, exhausted and embarrassed by her speech.

The therapist nods and glances through her file before speaking again.

'I see that bi-polar has been mentioned,' she murmurs as she reads. Looking up from the file she continues in an explanatory fashion.

'That condition involves severe high and low moods, changes in sleep, energy, thinking and behaviour. Someone with bi-polar will have periods of feeling overly happy and energised—hypermania is the medical term—and other periods of feeling incredibly sad, hopeless, and sluggish—that's known as

hypomania. Hypermania is worse of course as it's more overwhelming and there can be delusions and hallucinations, sleeping difficulties due to racing thoughts, lack of coping skills, poor decisions and a high sexual drive.'

She starts to panic. It was sounding far too familiar. The therapist continued to drone on.

'All of these symptoms are present in hypomania of course—excepting the delusions and hallucinations—but are far milder and they don't effect everyday life,' she pauses and adds casually, 'but I personally don't believe that you are bi-polar although you are definitely showing signs of hypomania.'

The therapist returns to the file again and produces a sheet with a basic diagram of the human brain printed on it. The diagram shows the neo cortex and the limbic cortex.

'I believe,' the therapist says referring to the sheet, 'that your problem is all to do with a fight between your new brain—the neo cortex—which is designed for analysis, planning, self-reflection, and self-monitoring; and your old brain—the limbic cortex, which is your "animal brain" and is designed for survival, fight or flight, avoidance, and shut-down.'

There is an awkward silence and when the therapist receives no verbal response to her theory, but simply another nod of the head, she continues to explain.

'Our old brain was designed to protect us—it isn't logical or rational. As I said, it is the part of the brain that controls fight or flight and all our emotions. Our new brain deals with planning, imagination, thinking and self-reflection. These two parts of the brain are connected, but I believe that you—for example when you're anxious—are getting stuck in your old brain. What you need to do is to get back into your new brain, to learn to access it so that you can self-reflect and calm yourself.'

Another awkward silence. She really doesn't know how to respond. She feels overwhelmed and a little confused.

'So,' the therapist continues undeterred, 'our new brain can be hi-jacked, shall we say, by our old brain. It gets hi-jacked by our fears and by threats. It makes us—you—focus on threat-based anxiety or anger.' She hesitates briefly. 'What I think we need to do is to make our goal to be training you to pull yourself back to your new brain. We need to get you to use your thinking and attention to control your unpleasant emotions and thoughts, and to instead stimulate positive emotions.'

'That would be great,' she says, wondering exactly how she is supposed to achieve this.

'A first simple step that may help you to do this is for you to have some structure in your daily routine,' the therapist resumes. 'Keeping a diary of sorts— a daily list of what you want or need to do, to plan ahead—it can help with stress management. You can mark off your achievements, and it will create a sense of positivity for you.'

'I do that already,' she responds, 'and I do find it helpful but if I don't achieve something that's on my to do list, if I can't tick something off, that causes a problem for me. That's when the panic can start again.'

'I see,' the therapist muses. 'So, it is a case of time management for you. I suggest that you learn to delegate and to allow sufficient time in which to complete your tasks and to prioritise what you feel to be essential. Allow flexibility, be aware that the unexpected can change our plans, pace yourself and try your best to finish what you start.'

'Ok, that sounds good,' she pauses, thinking. 'What you were saying before, about the brain, would that help with the other thing, with what happened to me when I was a child? It's all linked isn't it, what's happening to me now and what happened then...' She trails off.

'The child abuse?' the therapist responds abruptly. 'Yes, certainly. But I don't want to talk about that. Not that I don't think that it's important,' she adds quickly almost as an afterthought, 'but I don't believe that this is the correct space to discuss the matter. What do you think?'

'I don't really know,' she responds, confused. 'I just know that I want to stop thinking about it and remembering what happened. I don't want it to control me anymore.'

'Well, I think that we need to separate the two issues: emotional regulation and previous trauma,' the therapist says firmly. 'Yes, they are linked, and they will overlap, but I think we don't want to confuse the issues. So, I suggest that we find you a specialist to talk to about the child abuse. I believe that that would be more helpful for you. Is that ok?'

'Yes, ok. Whatever you think is best,' she acquiesces.

'Good. I'll look into that and get it sorted,' the therapist says, making a note in her diary. 'I'm not sure how long the wait will be—probably a few months at least—but I can get the ball rolling. You could also look into it yourself if you

like. In the meantime, try not to get stuck in that old brain. I'll see you the same time next week.'

And with that she is sent back into the labyrinth once more.

Thoughts

I came really hard thinking of you last night. That's what he told me. And I told him that I would make him come even harder. I will be on my back, and he will kiss my lips, my neck, my breasts. Then he will move his hand down and put his fingers inside me until I come. If I am happy with him, I will allow him to sit gently on my chest and put his cock in my mouth. I'll suck him and lick him and bite him. Then he will enter me, hard and firm. He'll be gentle at first then fiercer and faster until we both come together.

Fairy story.

The Woman

We need to talk. I don't want to lie to you. There's someone else. I slept with her last night.

You bastard! I risked everything for you. I can't believe that you'd do this to me again. Who is she? I thought that you loved me.

Pull yourself together. After all these years, you still ask if I love you?

I hate you so much right now.

I'm sorry. I don't know what else to say to you.

Just tell me the truth.

I feel under a lot of pressure. Nothing changes with you. I don't see a happy ending for us, just trouble. And you are so confused, one day you want one thing and the next day something else.

Can we meet? Talk about this face to face? Or are you ending things with me?

I need a few days to figure this all out. I need time to work out what to do. I'm sorry.

Thoughts

We visit. We talk. No sex. Apparently now advance warning is needed. We hug. We kiss, gently, tentatively. *'We are starting over—'* I think. Is that your penis I feel hardening against me? It's a shame about the advance warning— you're missing out on sexy undies. And more. But you say that you are fed up

with games. I'm not playing games though. I never was playing. It was more than that for me.

But he says that we are still friends. That we always will be. He will always be there for me. I love you so much. I love you too, he says. But...

Always a "but". He says that we are on different paths. I thought he wanted to take things to the next level. To make things more serious, more concrete. I thought you cared. But now you say that there is someone else, that you slept with her. You even show me her picture. You brag about her. I can't compete, not with her, a younger and more attractive version of me. I thought that I meant something to you. I feel so stupid. I believed you when you said that you loved me. I meant it.

Do you want me as a lover? A friend? Neither? Help me to understand. I promise that there will be no more ifs and buts this time.

You're laughing at me. Don't laugh at me.

Fuck you.

XIX
The Beginning of the End

The Patient

The man sits opposite across the table from her, and glances perfunctorily through her file. After what feels like a lifetime, he finally acknowledges her existence, briefly looking up at her and giving his name. Another day and yet another psychiatrist.

'So, how have you been?' he asks, his pen poised over a sheet of paper.

'Not too bad, I guess. I'm still having panic attacks and—' she begins but is rudely interrupted.

'Yes, yes,' he responds irritably.

'They worry me,' she persists. 'I lose time and I don't know what's happening. Can you help me?'

'I have questions to ask you,' he responds sternly, blatantly ignoring her obvious plea for assistance. 'How is your mood?'

'Sometimes it's ok, sometimes it's not,' she answers honestly. 'I have days where I'm euphoric and they should be good days, but they scare me because I know that I'm just going to hit rock bottom.'

'What do you mean?' he enquires, but he does not sound or look particularly interested.

'I mean that I feel that I just go from one extreme emotion to another,' she answers.

'How long would each emotion last?' he asks. He is still writing, and he does not look up from his paper as he asks her this question.

'It depends.' She feels nervous, she doesn't like eye contact, but this is almost worse, it is as if she is not even present in the room. She feels as if she is talking to a machine.

'Sometimes a day, sometimes a week…' She trails off.

'Is there anyone with bi-polar disorder in your family?' he asks bluntly, still refusing to look up from what he is writing.

'No. Not that I know of,' she replies.

'And sleeping?' he asks, still not making eye contact.

'I don't,' she says. 'Well, not really, I'm—'

'Yes, yes,' he interrupts. He sounds irritated again. 'Anything else?'

'Well, there's the voice,' she begins timidly. 'That—'

'It is just your inner voice,' he interjects forcefully. He obviously does not want to discuss this, or anything else for that matter, but at least he is now looking at her.

'But it tells me do things,' she begins. She doesn't like the pleading, the whine, that is beginning to creep into her voice.

'Like what?' he sighs.

'To hurt myself,' she mumbles, almost inaudibly, frightened to admit the truth to this man. 'To kill myself.'

'And have you?' he asks tersely. 'Hurt yourself? Or tried to commit suicide?'

She feels like she is being admonished.

'Yes,' she whispers.

He pauses in his interrogation and makes some more notes.

'Can you help me?' she pleads.

'No,' he says brusquely.

'Give be some advice then?' she implores.

'It's not my speciality,' he says curtly, his eyes firmly focused on his papers once more. 'I am just here to ask a few questions and to check that your medication is working. You will get another appointment to discuss any other issues.'

She sits in stunned silence, unsure of what she should say, as he glances through her file.

'Keep taking your current medication,' he continues without looking up. 'You will get another appointment shortly.'

He shuffles his notes together and leaves the room without a backward glance, leaving her sat in her chair.

A few days later a letter arrives in the post. It is regarding her appointment to discuss her "issues" with her usual psychiatrist. The appointment is for six months' time.

The Woman

I don't remember what sex is. We don't make love anymore.

That's because you don't do what I tell you. You have to mind-fuck him all the time. You have to be in control of everything, from money to his cock. If you had listened to me, you would have two men anytime that you wanted, but

instead you are at home and frustrated. I gave you the means, but no. You choose this. That's why I don't see a future for us.

You have to take my situation into account. It's hard.

Right. But you don't take me and my feelings into account, do you? Just live your life the way you want, but don't complain to me anymore if you're not going to do anything. I've seen enough.

I'm doing my best. I am trying.

You don't really get it, do you? You're supposed to be in charge and tell him what to do. Never mind. You will always be there in this same situation. The only difference will be is that I won't be watching anymore.

I'm working on my assertiveness. What exactly do you want from me?

That is exactly my point. After all this time and all of our chats, you still don't have any idea what my thoughts are. With this in mind, I am starting to want exactly nothing from you.

I do know what your thoughts are! You want me to be assertive, to do things for me, to stand up for myself, to be the best version of me. I am trying. But if I can accept you for you, why can't you do the same for me?

Because sadly, you don't have a clue who I am.

I'm sure I do, but please help me if you think otherwise.

There's no point. Forget about it. Stop loving me and start loving yourself.

I will, I promise. But I can love us both. You could try loving me back.

I don't care anymore.

You said that we would always be ok and now you don't care about me?

Both those statements are correct in the sense that I am still hoping to see some changes in your life but also if you want me in your life you have to make an effort. But all I see is submission. There are loads of ifs and buts, but the thing is I need to think about me too. I have to be better. I need to be better. With you, it's the same stuff all the time. Nothing changes. But it's not up to me to expect more from you. It's not right for me to want you to change. You're an adult and you may live your life the way you know and can. It's your life at the end of the day, and if you're happy with it then you need to leave me alone.

Please. I need you.

You said once that if at some stage you weren't enough for me, then that would be ok: you would walk away. I am telling you now: you are not enough for me in your current version. You give me nothing, but I am expected to always be at your disposal. I won't be at your disposal anymore.

Thoughts

Why didn't I stand up for myself? Why was I crying? I don't understand. If you love someone, then you should want them to be happy. He said once that I was perfect. He said I had everything, that I am beautiful, intelligent, sexy. He said he would always be my friend, that he would always be there for me. So why is it like this now? Why does life have to be so hard? It's all my fault, it has to be. I am a lost cause. I might as well end it all now, jump in the river, slit my wrists. Anything to stop feeling like this. To stop feeling so lost and worthless.

No. I mustn't say that. He doesn't like it when I say things like that. He wants a strong, independent woman by his side. Like I used to be. But I'm not the same as when we first met and that's a problem apparently. But of course I'm not the same, and neither is he. Life continually changes all of us. I have changed, but has that change made me stronger or weaker as a person?

He doesn't understand. You want me to change? To tell everyone that I'm seeing you? Is that it? To really fuck everyone over? Will that make me strong and independent in your eyes? Or is this just your way of really saying goodbye, of forcing me out of your life without a guilty conscience—or at least with not much of one.

It's all my fault. I know this. I obsess and I fantasise, and I destroy every little chance of happiness that comes my way. I torment and I hurt the people I love on a continuous basis. Forever a let-down. What is wrong with me? Why am I always making things worse? How can I change, become a better person? I will be punished, I know this. There are always consequences for our actions, that is a certainty. What goes around comes around. Destiny. Karma. Fate. Call it what you will. It might me be, it might be someone near me—someone that I love—but it will happen: retribution will be meted, and I will pay penance, I will be held to account. Things will start to go wrong. People will get ill or hurt. And it will all be my fault. Everything is always because of me; I can't do right for doing wrong. I've been told enough times by so many people that I need to change, that I need to be a better person. I should have listened. I should have made things right. Now it seems too late, I don't know what to do or how to do it. I am so confused, and I need peace and quiet to try and sort things out. Please. Stop. Talking.

You are the root cause of it all, you and your stupid thoughts and feelings. You trigger everything bad that happens in your life. You need to stop. You need to put an end to all this pain and suffering. But I bet you can't even do that, can

you? You are too selfish, too much of a coward. You always have been. It is all your fault. You know this. You obsess, you fantasise, and you destroy every possibility of happiness that you have ever had.

But it is time to listen now. I keep telling you what you have to do to make things right, to act for the greater good for once in your life. You cause pain. You cause grief. No one needs you anymore and no one wants you that's for sure. You are surplus to requirements. Past your use by date. You have always made the wrong choices. Make the right one now. Kill yourself. It's time to die.

The Patient

Her therapist ushers her into a different room, saying that because this one is more secluded it will be more appropriate for their sessions. She has been talking about embarking on some Eye Movement Desensitisation and Reprocessing, or EMDR, a non-traditional and somewhat controversial type of psychotherapy used in particular to treat post-traumatic stress disorder. The therapist has been attending a course and she obviously wants a guinea pig on whom to try out her knew ideas and to hone her skills on. There will be no more talk therapy for a while and eventually no more medication. Instead, rapid, rhythmic eye movements will be used to approach and relieve psychological issues. To her it sounds like a sure-fire way of bringing on a migraine to which she has always been prone, but the therapist is so excited to try out the new technique that she does not have the heart to say this and to refuse to try the new therapy.

The new room is bright and spacious with the usual table and two chairs on opposing sides, but unusually these chairs are padded and soft and relatively comfortable. A window looks out onto a courtyard filled with white roses. They sit.

'So, how are you?' the therapist asks. Four simple words, the usual preamble to the opening of a session but more kindness than she has heard in such a long time. The tears begin to stream down her face, smearing her cheap mascara and rendering her eyes bloodshot. Embarrassed by her show of emotion, she wipes the tears clumsily away before she replies.

'I can't do this anymore, this pretence. It's all too much,' she sobs incoherently.

The therapist pushes a box of tissues across the table to her and waits patiently for the tears to subside and to hear more. Dabbing her eyes and stifling her tears she continues, filling the silence.

'I just want it all to end. I can't do right for doing wrong. I destroy everything,' she says, the sobs beginning to rack her chest once more as her hysteria rises.

'Tell me what happened,' the therapist asks softly.

'I don't know exactly. I can't remember,' she moans. 'I don't know what's real or what's not anymore. I don't know what's happening. But he says that I have to be punished! That there will be consequences for my actions. I'm so scared.'

Another fit of sobs convulses her, and she covers her face with her hands and pulls roughly at her hair.

'Go to your safe place,' the therapist soothes. 'It's all going to be all right. Remember: what happened in the past was the past. We must not let it affect how you act and how you respond to situations now. You are not that submissive little girl anymore.'

'I know,' she gasps, attempting to smother her tears and be coherent. 'I just want everyone to be happy, for everyone to be ok, but everything I do hurts them.'

'And what about you?' the therapist enquires. 'What about your happiness?'

There is no response to this question, so the therapist tries another tack.

'What would make you happy?' she asks, but a shrug of the shoulders is the only response to this question.

'Ok,' the therapist perseveres. 'What exactly is worrying you? What has stressed you out today?'

The direct approach works and finally there is a response.

'That I have no friends, no life, I have nothing to look forward to and my time is running out. No one loves me, not really,' she pauses, fighting back the tears. 'I ruin everything.'

'So, realistically, what can you do about that?' the therapist responds.

'I don't know,' she answers. 'I guess I don't really need friends.'

'No,' the therapist responds firmly. 'That is the little girl talking. You do not have to be submissive. You can find new friends. You have to start doing things just for you for a change. Join a club or a gym. Find something that gives you joy, that allows you to achieve. You have to put you first. There has to be self-compassion.'

'I suppose I could ask if I could—' she begins but the therapist interrupts before she can finish her sentence.

'You do not need to ask for anyone's permission. You are a grown woman and you are doing no harm,' she says resolutely.

She nods feebly, wiping away her tears on the now sodden tissue, tears which show no sign of relenting. The therapist continues.

'It is all about the emotional mind, the wise mind and the reasonable mind,' she says. 'Do you remember we have talked about that?'

Another nod before the therapist resumes.

'When you are feeling overwhelmed, or stressed, or finding a situation difficult, I want you to stop and take a breath,' the therapist says calmly. 'Use your wise mind and think about what is going on. Put in some perspective—what are you reacting to, is it a fact or an opinion, how would someone else see it. Then make your decision, your response. Do you think that you can do that, or at least try?'

Another nod.

'At the very least, when you are feeling overwhelmed, go to your safe place. That is always there for you,' she taps the side of her head and smiles. A quick glance at her watch indicates that time is up. The session is over.

'Well! We've over-run!' the therapist laughs. They both stand to leave and as they do the therapist picks up a sheet of paper from the pile on the table and folds it in half.

'I almost forgot,' she says proffering the folded sheet. 'It's on the subject of self-care. Have a look at it over the coming days, it might be of help.'

She takes the piece of paper and they both walk to the door.

'I shall see you next week,' the therapist says, and then as an afterthought to the receding back of her patient, 'and make sure that you hug your inner child!'

*

Safely ensconced behind the wheel of her car, she unfolds the sheet of paper and glances at it. It is entitled "The Compassionate Kit: Your Survival Kit for Life". It suggests collecting meaningful items that would nourish your compassionate self. These meaningful items should be placed in a special box, and they should make you feel good about yourself and bring you strength, calm, confidence, and wisdom. Apparently, this "Compassionate Kit" should be kept nearby, or even on your person, so that you can remind yourself on a daily basis of all the good things about yourself and see reminders of things that make you

happy. It all seemed a little too new-age hippy for her taste but she continued to read. Next came suggestions for what one should consider placing in the special box. The suggestions included music, pictures, smells, books, quotes, objects of meaning, a hobby, reminders of strengths, grounding or soothing objects, a letter from your compassionate self. She paused to consider what she had read. What would she put in such a box? Some dried lavender perhaps, a smooth pebble, a book maybe—but which one? No, forget a book, there were just far too many to choose from. What was that last suggestion—a letter from your compassionate self. Definitely not. She didn't think that she could manage that, she wasn't even sure what a "compassionate self" was and was inclined to think that she probably didn't have one, but it did remind her of something that the therapist had suggested a few sessions ago and that she had, of course, completely disregarded. The suggestion had been that she should write a letter to her childhood abuser, to get all of her thoughts, feelings, and emotions down on paper. It was supposed to be a cathartic exercise. By writing this letter, she would apparently be able to purge her spirit, to release all the pain and hurt, and be cleansed and liberated. Maybe she would be purified, healed by writing such a letter. *'Could a letter like that go in the box if I wrote it,'* she wondered? Would such a letter be inspiring and make her feel stronger—less of a victim—or would it simply bring back too many painful memories and push her deeper into her dark space. It was worth considering however. Perhaps writing this letter could be this weeks self-imposed homework.

The Wife

Her cognitive behavioural therapy homework this week is to write a letter to her childhood abuser. She does not think that she will be able to do this, and she does not entirely see the point in the exercise, but as sleep is evading her, she may as well give it a try. She gets a pen and paper and settles comfortably in the corner of the couch. She didn't think that she could do this, but once the pen hits the paper, she cannot stop.

I am writing to you because for far too many years, I have kept what you did to me bottled up inside and I don't want to do that anymore. I know that you remember, but like me you choose to ignore it. I can't—I won't—ignore it anymore. In the past couple of years, what you did to me has pushed itself forward and I am finding it increasingly difficult to ignore it all. Perhaps in the

end, this will be helpful, acknowledging all the horrible things that you did to me over the years. It might help me to understand myself better and help me to be a better person. Perhaps it will be therapeutic, cathartic. But I want it to be therapeutic and cathartic for me: I don't want that for you. So let me be clear: I am writing this letter to help me, *not you. I do not want an apology from you—I can never forgive you. Nor do I want any explanations or excuses from you— they would be lies, meaningless—and just another way for you to try and control me and compound my guilt at having participated in your "games" for all those years.*

I know what you did to me. I know that you probably did the same to others. I know, from what I have heard, that you have—and maybe still are—playing your "games" with your own children. You are evil. You make my flesh crawl. You make me feel dirty and stupid, even now. And I don't like admitting that to you as I don't want you to have any feelings of power over me. I don't want you to continue to enjoy my suffering—because I have suffered, and I still suffer even though I have a husband and a child and a lovely home.

You subjected me to years of abuse from the age of five or six to the age of eleven. You took away my childhood. My innocence. I used to make a lovely den for myself, I used to love to pretend that it was my own little house—a safe refuge. But you spoiled all of that. I was about five. You were a teenager. You would come inside to "play". Your choice of games would either be schools or mummies and daddies. Both games always involved learning about the body. It's one of my earliest memories, you making me put my hands in your knickers, making me put my fingers inside you. I remember how it felt. I remember how much I hated it. I remember not understanding what we were playing. But I trusted you.

Those type of games went on for years. In my father's shed, you would lay me on the ground, you on top of me, both of us naked. You had "movie nights", the curtains drawn and a blanket over our laps, and you would touch me and make me touch you. There are still certain movies, certain songs, that I can't bear to watch or to hear.

You liked to play "doctors and nurses" when I was older, I was about nine or ten. You invited your friends to join in that game. I was always the patient and you subjected me to your own style of examination, fingers and tongue probing every inch of me and every orifice. I can't remember what your friends did, that

man...I hope that I haven't blocked out something worse. That is one thing I would like an answer to.

Worst of all were the night-times. All those years of being afraid to sleep because more often than not, you would slip into my bed. You would touch me, put your fingers inside me. Make me do the same to you. I didn't want to. I didn't like it. I didn't understand. I was only little when it started. I guess that I just wanted to please you. I trusted you. I thought that it must be ok, even if I didn't like it. When I got older, I would pretend to be asleep, I would curl into the wall. But it didn't stop you.

Maybe none of this seems wrong to you. Maybe you think that because we kept up some sort of pretence for my parents' sake for all these years that I am ok with it all, that it didn't affect me. But it did and it still does. Don't you remember my night terrors? My panic attacks? My dissociation episodes? They all started when I was about six and have continued all my life.

And what about a small child continually getting thrush? Or an eight-year-old not speaking for over a year?

I still suffer from panic attacks as I did as a child and a teenager. I still have dissociation and derealisation episodes. I still have nightmares and difficulty sleeping. I take so many tablets now, but they don't truly help.

As a young adult, I felt dirty being intimate with my husband and I felt guilty if I enjoyed it. I also never realised that I was allowed to say "no". As an adult, I believe that I don't deserve to feel good about myself. I blame all of this on you, and I am right to do so. You made me compliant in your sick little games. You made me submissive and weak. A victim.

Do you remember when I confronted you about all this? I was about eleven. I tried to strangle you. I told you then a little about how I feel, about you and what you had done to me. You just laughed. And so, I buried everything. Every memory, every emotion, every feeling. I never spoke about it again until now. And I feel so guilty about not speaking up before because I know that I wasn't the last to be made to play your games.

I remember when your own daughter turned five, you told me that you thought that she was me, you even called her by my name sometimes. I have watched your children suffer and I have done nothing. I have watched the light and life disappear from their eyes just as it did from mine. I have watched on unknown by you as you have caressed and fondled your own son. And I did nothing. I should have helped but I can barely help myself. How I feel is

consuming me and I know that I have to stop thinking about it, but the fact is it is now a part of me, it will always affect me no matter what. I don't want anything from you—I hate you; you disgust me—but please, no more.

The letter was never sent. The weighted chain that had held her so tightly loosened for a little while, but it was never cast off. It would always be there, holding her back, threatening to drag her down and engulf her in the darkness.

Thoughts

He said: you know what, let's take a break for a few years and see what happens.

But he said nothing would happen and that he has had enough of this stupid game.

He said there is too much information about things he doesn't care about. Like child molestation.

He said that nothing will ever change and that this is not something that makes him feel good. It annoys him.

So he doesn't need me in his life anymore. He said he has enough shit in his life already and he doesn't need more. I don't give him anything, I am more hassle than joy.

He said: it's the same thing over and over again and I am still debating whether this—whatever it is—is worth my time and attention.

So he's better off without me.

So no one needs me.

He said that he has had to put up with loads of my crap and has had to witness all my downs.

He said: I don't see any progress and I don't think that things will ever change, therefore whatever it is that we have, it is pointless.

He said that he doesn't even think that I want to change anything, that all I have are thoughts—only thoughts and nothing in reality.

He said that he doesn't want to see me once in a blue moon when I can escape my real world. He doesn't want an occasional phone call or an occasional text.

I am to leave him alone.

He said he doesn't want to be my daydream anymore.

I am bad news.

He said: I don't even know who you are.

He said that he needs a sane and driven person around him, and he questions himself—is that me?

He hopes that I will understand if at some point he disappears from my virtual control.

He said that he is thinking of himself. That he has to.

He said: I don't see you bringing anything good into my life.

He said: live your life the way you want and live it without me.

Then he said goodbye.

It's a little heads up.

So you know why I disappeared.

XX
The Sum of all Parts

She put the finished letter down on the coffee table beside the couch. Cognitive Behavioural Therapy homework all finished. She had surprised herself. Now what? She glanced at her old diary lying beside her wedding album on the couch where she had discarded them earlier. She contemplated her next move. She would leave the letter and the diary open here on the coffee table, alongside the half empty bottle of whisky and her medication, where they could not be failed to be found. Then she picked up her pen and began to write once more.

Dear Diary,
I'm not very good at saying goodbye. I wish that you had seen the real me, the whole me. I am so much more than you think I am.
I'm sure that you know by now how much I love you and need you. Without you I am nothing. I did imagine a different goodbye with you, but I guess that's life, we never get exactly what we want do we?
I am so sorry, but this life is just too much for me and you will be so much better without me.
Take care of yourself.
Goodbye.

X

CPSIA information can be obtained
at www.ICGtesting.com
Printed in the USA
LVHW051653280523
748262LV00004B/180